School For Spirits: Angel of Death

Spirit School, Volume 4

Aron Lewes

Published by Aron Lewes, 2019.

SCHOOL FOR SPIRITS: ANGEL OF DEATH

First edition. January 30, 2019.

ISBN: 979-8215816233

Written by Aron Lewes.

Author's Notes

MY DAD HAD DEMENTIA. With each passing day, I saw him lose more and more himself, until there was barely anything left of the man I once knew. For two years, my sister and I were his caregivers. Those were easily the most turbulent two years of my life.

In April 2017, we made a gut-wrenching decision. My sisters and I decided it was time to move Dad into a rest home. By then, he couldn't remember who we were.

During this difficult time, I started writing my first *School for Spirits* book. In it, Taishi Nakamura places a hand on the forehead of a man with dementia, and the man suddenly remembers his daughters. I wrote this book around June-August of 2017.

In October of that year, we got a call from my dad's rest home: he had been moved to the hospital. When my sisters and I visited him that night, we were stunned. Dad remembered us. He remembered our names! He remembered the names of actors on tv. He was even cracking jokes like our old dad used to!

We were amazed. We thought we had him back!

Two weeks later, he passed away.

I kept thinking about *School for Spirits* and Taishi. It was as if I'd predicted my own life before it happened. I like to think I had my own Taishi Nakamura who blessed me with few more days with my father.

I'm not as young as Lucy, this novel's heroine, but I have something in common with her. Like her, I've experienced a lot of death at a fairly young age. Several parts of *"Angel of Death"* are based on true events.

I think death is probably the most difficult thing a person can go through. You never fully recover from losing a loved one. If you've lost someone too, my heart goes out to you, and I hope this book gives you some comfort.

-Aron

Chapter One

WHEN MOST STUDENTS graduate from spirit school, they say goodbye to their instructor and look for a new partner. Not me. The day after I finish my fifth and final mission, I get a mysterious message from Amber.

Come to the classroom tomorrow, Luciana. Do not go on any more missions. Thank you.

The message doesn't tell me much, but it doesn't sound promising. Was I so bad at my missions that I'm not allowed to take any more?

My instructor was a sixty-six-year-old former Chicago gangster named Larry. For a gangster, he was a surprisingly nice guy, but he didn't have much in common with an eighteen-year-old Hispanic girl from Los Angeles. To be honest, he scared me a little. His hair was always slicked back, he had ice cold eyes, and he dressed like he was auditioning for a *Godfather* movie. Still, we managed to complete four out of five missions, leaving me with a respectable grade. My grandma said she only completed two of her missions when she was in spirit school. Three is average, I guess. If I did slightly better than average, why is Amber calling me back to the classroom? I don't understand. Did I do something wrong?

I head to the classroom the next day, as directed. My dark brown hair is swinging in a high ponytail, I'm in a fuzzy yellow cardigan, and I've got a pair of freshly manifested Mary Janes on my feet. Before I left the house, Grandma said I looked like a librarian. As a lover of books, I take that as a compliment.

"Hello, Amber!" I greet my favorite angel with a smile and a wave. To be fair, she's the only angel I know, so she's my favorite by default. How could anyone *not* like Amber, though? She's so sweet.

"Hello, Lucy. You may sit anywhere you like," Amber says, motioning toward the sea of empty chairs. It's strange to see the classroom so empty. The last time I was here, it was filled with people of all ages and races.

I choose a seat in the middle of the room and widen my smile. Even if Amber has bad news for me, I'm determined to keep smiling. If I can smile through three years of cancer, I can smile through anything.

"So... you were probably confused by my message," Amber says.

"Yeah. *Very* confused," I tell her. "You don't want me to go on any more missions?" If I can't go on any more missions, that's a shame, because I was really looking forward to working with Mom and Grandma and Grandpa.

"It's okay. You haven't done anything wrong," Amber reassures me. "Actually, I was going to offer you a special assignment. Every so often, Archangel Azrael requests a new psychopomp. I thought you'd be a good candidate."

"What's a psychopomp?" I ask.

"A psychopomp escorts the souls of the dead to the spirit world. They have other names as well. Helpers. Deathbringers... I hate that name, though. It sounds so dark."

"When I died, you took me *Home*," I point out. "Does that mean you're one of those... psychopomps?"

"No. Other spirits can take the newly-deceased to the afterlife, but psychopomps deal *only* in death. It's a difficult job," Amber says. "I thought I would offer you the position, Lucy. If you're interested, you would have to undergo a few weeks of training with Archangel Azrael. Normally, this opportunity is only presented to students who complete all five of their missions, but you're a special case. You've seen a lot of death at such a young age."

She's definitely not wrong about that. When I was really little, I used to ride on my grandpa's shoulders. He built a dollhouse for me, fixed my broken bike, and we watched cartoons every weekend. He was the best friend I could have ever wanted—and he died when I was ten. Grandma died a year later. When I was thirteen, my mom died in a car accident. A week after my Quinceañera, I was diagnosed with cancer. Now, three years later, I'm dead too. I was a survivor, though. I outlived every doctor's prediction.

Death has followed me forever. It's not all bad, though. I've been reunited with the abuelos I love so much, and Mom and I live together again. I miss my dad and brother, though. It sucks that they're all alone now.

"So, Lucy, what do you think?" Amber asks. "Would you be interested?"

"I guess so." I wonder if I should sound more enthusiastic. It's probably an honor to work with an Archangel.

"Good. Have you heard of the Hill of Black Roses? That's where Azrael would like to meet you. He—" Amber pauses to check a message on her LightTab. "Well, it looks like he's busy for the next few hours. I'll send you another message to let you know when he's ready for you."

"Okay." When Amber doesn't say anything else, I start eying the door. "Is that all you needed me for?"

Amber replies, "Yes, dear, you're free to go. Like I said, I'll contact you in a bit."

I guess I have a few hours to kill, so I head back to the house I share with Mom. She's away on a mission right now, so I have the place to myself. I flop down on the living room couch to do some research on psychopomps. It really does sound like a tough job. One former candidate described her training as *emotional torture.*

I unearth *tons* of pics of Archangel Azrael on the LightTab. There are pictures of him in a leather coat, pictures of him on a motorcycle, pictures of him with short hair, pictures of him with long hair. I even find some shirtless pictures of him. His body isn't bad, but he's a bit skinny for my liking.

Dios mio, he has a *lot* of fans. As I read through comments on a message board, I can feel myself blushing. There are a bunch of girls—and guys, I assume—who want to do unspeakable things to him. He's often described as a "sexy bad boy," but I wonder if he's really that bad? Maybe they're judging him because he's the Angel of Death? His title makes him sound like a dark and tragic figure.

One site refers to Azrael as *"the only Archangel as popular as Michael."* After an hour of research, I come to the same conclusion. Azrael has a pretty rabid fan base—and I'm going to meet him soon.

I thought I'd have a chance to talk to Mom about this psychopomp stuff before Amber contacted me again, but I'm wrong.

Archangel Azrael would like to speak to you now. Meet him on the Hill of Black Roses.

My stomach does a tumble when I read that. I shouldn't have read so much about Azrael, because now I'm *really* nervous. Now I feel like I'm meeting an idol.

I can't warp yet. If I could, I could get to our meeting place in a flash, but I have to walk there. Fortunately, it's not too far away. I find my way using a LightTab map, and when I arrive, there's no doubt I'm at the right place. I've never seen a black rose before. Here, there are thousands of them. There are so many, I can barely see the red grass growing between them.

Black roses and red grass. What a strange place.

At the top of the hill, I find Archangel Azrael. He's all alone, sitting on the ground with his eyes closed and his legs crossed. There's a giant sword in his lap, and he appears to be meditating. I don't want to alarm him, so I clear my throat as I approach.

His eyes slowly open, and he studies me with the blankest expression I've ever seen. His eyes are really strange, actually. His left eye is deep blue, and the right eye is a blackish red color. I didn't notice that when I was looking at pictures of him, but now that I see him up close, it's kind of spooky.

When he doesn't say anything, I decide to introduce myself. "Um... h-hi. I'm Luciana Alvarez. Amber said I was supposed to meet you here?"

"I know who you are, Ms. Alvarez." Azrael's voice is soft and deep, almost a bit chilling.

"Uh... good." I try to smile at him, but his expression stays blank. "So, you were looking for a new psychopomp?"

"I prefer to call them Helpers," Azrael says. "But... yes. I am looking for one. I don't know if you'd be right for the job, though. You look... soft."

I guess *soft* isn't the worst insult I've ever heard. There are worse ways he could've described me.

"Hey, I'm pretty tough!" I defend myself. "I lived with cancer for three years! I was only supposed to live for one."

He just stares at me, expressionless and unblinking. Is he expecting me to say something else? Am I supposed to audition?

Azrael finally says, "Being a Helper will break you. I know your type. You have to be *incredibly strong* or this job will break you." Before I can think of a good defense, he adds, "However, I will defer to Amber's judgment and give you a chance."

"Is there anything you want to know about me?" I ask.

"Not especially," Azrael answers with a sigh. "I'm sorry if that sounds cold."

"It does!" I exclaim. "My last instructor was a gangster, and even he took the time to get to know me a little bit!"

"Anything you could tell me about yourself is just a secondhand opinion. I would rather get to know you as we work together," Azrael says.

It's been all of two minutes, and I'm already trying to figure out why this guy's got so many fans. It must be his reputation—or his hair. He does have nice black hair.

When Azrael stands, I'm shocked by how tall he is. He's over six feet tall, and I'm barely over five, so he towers over me.

"Are you ready to get started, Ms. Alvarez?"

"Lucy," I correct him. "Just call me Lucy."

In a deadpan voice, he repeats, "Are you ready to get started, Ms. Alvarez?"

With a very obvious sneer on my face, I reply, "Sure."

As soon as his hand touches my arm, we leave the Hill of Roses behind.

Chapter Two

AZRAEL AND I WARP TO an eclectically decorated living room where two girls are streaming Netflix on a bright, striped couch. There's a huge cactus in the corner, a statue of the Pillsbury Dough Boy, and a chair shaped like a bear. Both girls have light brown hair and big blue eyes. They look similar enough that I wonder if they're sisters.

Azrael's standing beside me like a statue. With his ghostly pale skin and chiseled cheekbones, he looks like he *could* be made from marble. He hasn't said anything since we've arrived, so I ask, "If we're here, and we're supposed to take people to the afterlife... does that mean one of these girls is going to die?"

"Not exactly."

His vague answer makes me grunt. "Can you explain what you mean by that?"

Azrael says, "First, you need to understand that a Helper's missions are different than those of a regular spirit guide. We're not here to grant a wish, we're here to escort a soul to the other side. Once that's done, our mission is complete. However, should a dying charge have a final request, we can and should try to grant it."

"Okay." He still hasn't answered my question, but I'm trying not to get too annoyed. "Does that mean one of these girls is going to die, Azrael? Which one is our charge?"

"Our charge is Simone Teagarden, the one with the ponytail," Azrael says. "I should point out, Ms. Alvarez, that you are no longer a student, so this information should be automatically available on your

LightTab. You no longer need anyone to hold your hand and spell everything out to you."

A part of me wants to blow up at him, because he was *clearly* being rude, but I smile instead. That's my usual reaction when someone is a jerk to me. They expect a sassy retort, but a smile confuses them.

When I turn on my LightTab, a picture of Simone appears on the screen, as well as some stats about her. She's a twenty-four-year-old grocery store clerk living in Boise, Idaho, and she's pregnant. She's currently living with her older sister, Carmen. I assume that's the girl sitting next to her.

"Is Simone going to die?" I ask. I already feel a bit queasy about this. If being a "Helper" means you have to watch people die all the time, can I really handle that? Maybe Azrael's right. Maybe I'm too soft. Maybe I'm not cut out for this.

"As I said before... not exactly. Observe for yourself, and you'll soon discover the truth."

Okay, his cryptic crap is really getting on my nerves. *Smile, Lucy*, I tell myself. Everything's okay if you just keep smiling.

Simone pauses the movie, claiming she needs to visit the restroom. When she gets up, I notice something strange. There's a small patch of blood between her legs. Even though her sweatpants are light gray, her sister doesn't seem to notice.

Panicked, Simone charges to the bathroom as fast as she can. I consider myself an empath, so I can feel her fear as if it was my own. We both know what's happening, and it isn't good.

"She's losing the baby," Azrael calmly states. "She's known it for awhile now. This isn't the first time she's bled."

"Why is your voice so... hollow? Don't you care at all?"

"I've been doing this for many years, Ms. Alvarez. I *do* care. I care more than you can imagine. However... I have to detach myself from every mission, or I would lose my mind. Work with me for awhile, and you'll start to understand."

"Do you definitely know she's losing the baby?" I ask.

"It's almost a certainty. That's why we're here."

"Well... is there anything we can do to help?"

Azrael, stony and stoic, faces the bathroom door. He's waiting for Simone to reemerge, I guess. "The situation would require a miracle. Have you had any experience with miracles?"

I shake my head. "Miracles? No."

"All Archangels and most angels can perform miracles, but they require approval from the Council," Azrael says. "I rarely request one unless it seems absolutely necessary. The best way we can help Ms. Teagarden is to be there for her. We support her. We remain at her side and help her through her inevitable grief."

I want to protest, but this is my first mission as Azrael's trainee, and I don't want to mess anything up. I already know why we're here. We're not here to help. We're not really "Helpers." We're not here to save lives, we're here to take them.

I already hate this job.

Azrael says, "Grief, in my opinion, is an important part of a human's growth. It deepens them. Strengthens them. As tragic as this is, she will grow and learn from it."

I reject his thoughts with a snort. "I don't agree. It'd be better to live in a world where people only know joy. Life shouldn't have to be difficult."

"If that's your opinion, quit now. You will *only* know grief if you work with me."

Amber thought I could do this, right? I don't want to let her down, so I should try to bury my feelings—for now, at least.

Simone's been in the bathroom for a long time. I can only imagine how scared she must be.

"Do you know if she has a boyfriend?" I almost say *baby daddy*, but I honestly don't know if an Archangel would be familiar with the term.

"The man who impregnated her is gone now, if that's what you're asking. He was her boyfriend, but he abandoned her two months ago. Simone is on her own."

"Well, she has her sister. Sometimes, a sister's love is all you need." *Or a brother.* My own brother got me through some really rough times.

"And her parents, I'm sure, will be concerned about her health," Azrael adds. "I didn't mean to imply there is no one who loves Simone. I only meant to point out there will only be one grieving parent in this scenario."

"Men are jerks." The opinion accidentally slips out of my mouth. "Not all of them, of course... but if the guy in her life just disappeared on her, that's not cool. What kind of a guy would leave his pregnant girlfriend?"

When Simone returns from the bathroom, she's wearing a different pair of pants. I wonder if her sister will notice the wardrobe change? Simone knows there's something wrong with her, but for some reason, she's trying to hide it.

"Why hasn't she talked to her sister about this?" I ask.

"I don't know. Would you like me to read her mind?" After a pause, he adds, "I mean that literally, not sarcastically."

Of course he didn't mean it sarcastically. I've known Azrael for less than an hour, but it would already surprise me if he was capable of sarcasm. He's so serious, and he never has any inflection in his voice.

"No, don't read her mind. That seems kind of intrusive. That seems like a—"

I'm too distracted to finish my thought.

Before she reaches the couch, Simone faints.

Chapter Three

AZRAEL AND I ACCOMPANY Simone and her sister to the hospital. She's in the ER first, then she's moved to one of the rooms. There, we await the inevitable bad news.

Simone's mom and dad are here, as well as Carmen. They've made a circle of chairs around her bed.

To lighten the mood, Simone's dad tries to crack a joke. All of a sudden, he blurts, "You know, I can see myself working in a mirror factory." It takes them a moment to digest it, and when they do, all the ladies groan.

"Ugh, that's such a dad joke!" Carmen whines.

"Well, I *am* a dad," he points out. "Anyway, *on reflection*, I thought it was pretty funny..."

When I glance at Azrael, his eyes are closed again, so I crack a joke of my own. "Did Simone's dad just bore you to sleep with his bad jokes?"

"No. I'm listening," Azrael says. "I can hear the baby's heartbeat. I hear it fading. Soon, there will be silence."

A moment later, Azrael expands his wings and moves closer to Simone's bed. I'm surprised by the blinding whiteness of his wings. They're almost too bright to look at. I've seen other angels' wings before, and they vary in color. Azrael's wings are, by far, the brightest I've seen.

Azrael knows the exact moment when the baby is lost—he knows before Simone and her family. He brings his hand to Simone's stomach, not quite touching her. When his hand rises, so does the spirit of her unborn child. It looks like a baby, but tiny, with curled arms and slit-like eyes. Azrael wraps the child in an orb of light and sends it floating over to me, presumably so I can get a closer look.

"He'll be raised by angels now," Azrael says. "His mother already gave him a name. *Isaac.* He'll live with us, grow with us, and when the time comes, he'll be reunited with his mother in the afterlife."

I reply in a low voice, cracked by tears that I'm trying to hold back. "That's... kind of sad."

Azrael rejects my observation with a tutting tongue. "It's not sad. Many lost children become their parents' spirit guides. He'll grow up knowing his family, and one day, they'll know him."

I can't stop staring at the spirit of Simone's tiny baby. It's hovering in front of me, swaddled in Azrael's ball of golden light. I have so many questions in my head, and Azrael answers one of them before I can ask. I'm pretty sure that means he's reading my mind. Until I met Azrael, I hadn't spent much time with angels, but I've heard that most of them are telepathic.

Azrael says, "He'll remain in the ball of light until his nine months are up. After that, he'll be raised like any other baby. Some grow into adulthood, while others choose to remain as children until they're reunited with their parents."

When I dip a finger into the light surrounding Isaac, it's warm, and has an instant soothing effect on me. I'm trying absorb everything Azrael's telling me, but it's a lot to take in.

"Now... we can either take Isaac Home right away, or we can stay with Simone until she's heard the news," Azrael says. "Many times, I like to stick around to share some comforting words with my charges. They can't hear me, but I believe my words still help them."

I tell him I want to stay, if only because I'm curious to see Azrael in "comforting" mode. He's tall, dark and brooding. Looking at him, I wouldn't guess he was the sort of guy who was capable of consoling words.

As we wait for a doctor to arrive, Azrael tells me, "Simone already knows he's gone. She can't feel him moving. She wants to be wrong, but... she knows."

A little less than an hour later, her family is sent from the room, and Simone's suspicions are confirmed by one of the doctors. She'll now be delivering a dead baby. She's trying to hold it together while the doctor is speaking, but I can see the tears in her eyes. She's devastated, and my heart is breaking for her.

Simone doesn't cry until the doctor is out of the room. Stroking her stomach, she whispers, "I wanted you, Isaac. I really did. I wanted you *so* much."

Azrael stands beside her, and when she sobs, he slides an arm around her shoulders. "You'll always be his mother," he tells her. "Your little boy will grow up loving you, anticipating the moment when you can be together. I promise we'll take good care of him. You're a strong woman, Simone. You've always been strong, but it's okay to grieve. I know it hurts, and it will probably hurt forever, but you're not alone. Your mother, father, sister... your family loves you so much. You have angels and guides who love you and want the best for you. Cry as much as you need to cry, but know you're never alone."

Azrael's speech and Simone's tears have me dabbing my eyes. The spirit of Isaac is next to me, and I know he'll be okay, but it's a difficult scene to watch.

When Azrael wraps a wing around her and strokes her hair, Simone's tears stop, and she draws a strengthening breath. I didn't know what I expected from Azrael, but it definitely wasn't *this*. He's so tender and warm. If others could watch what I just watched, his bad boy reputation would be gone in an instant.

The next time he speaks, Azrael's voice has gone cold again. "Let's go, Miss Alvarez. I think Simone will be fine."

Azrael sends us rocketing through the cosmos, and a few seconds later, we're standing in a crowded nursery. It reminds me of a hospital nursery, but it's been decorated to look more like a home. There are at least twenty babies, each with their own crib. Azrael takes Isaac to the opposite end of the room, where several other unborn spirits are floating in cradles of light. He leaves Isaac with the rest of them and returns to me a moment later.

"Welcome to Asylum One," he says. "In the Asylums, young spirits are nurtured and reared by angel volunteers. This is the infant wing."

"Asylum... One," I repeat the words in a whisper. "Wait, how many Asylums are there?"

"Hundreds, unfortunately. Think about it. All around the world, there are children who die before their time. There is always a new child in the Asylum. *Always.*"

I take a moment to ponder that. I guess I never thought about what happened to spirits of children who die before a parent.

"Sometimes..." as he speaks, Azrael opens the nursery door and motions for me to exit, "there are spirit grandparents who are willing and able to act as guardian to their grandchildren. In such cases, the children live with their families instead of an Asylum."

The hallways of Asylum One look like a medieval castle, or possibly a cathedral. There's a mural of angels on the ceiling, and ambient torches line the walls.

As I follow him down fire lit corridors, I say, "This looks like it'd be a pretty cool place to grow up."

"It can be. We try to make it as pleasant as possible. We don't want these children to feel like orphans... because they're *not* orphans. They have mothers and fathers who miss and adore them."

Azrael leads me to a giant room with high ceilings and stained glass windows. This part of the Asylum *definitely* looks like a cathedral. There are about a dozen children in here, and an angel is teaching them how to paint.

"This is the classroom," Azrael says. "Naturally, children in the Asylum also need to learn and play."

"I was never in any classrooms that looked like *this*!" Slack-jawed, I stare at a golden statue of Archangel Michael. "How long do children stay in the Asylum? 'Til what age?" I hope he's not annoyed by all of my questions. If he was, I wouldn't be able to tell, because he's always looking blank and sounding bored.

"It varies. Typically, they stay until maturity, which is usually fifteen or sixteen. As I've said before, some choose to freeze their physical age until they're reunited with their parents, and those children usually stay in the Asylum until their reunion."

"This is a lot to take in." I sidle closer to the children and their canvases. A boy, no older than ten, is working on a landscape that's *way* better than anything I could paint. He's even adding texture to the trees to make them look super realistic. I'm impressed.

"I hope you've been paying attention, because if you choose to become a Helper, you will have to manage an Asylum of your own," Azrael says. "But... it might be too soon to tell you that. I don't know if you've chosen to continue your lessons. Bear in mind, every day will be like this. I won't lie to you, Ms. Alvarez. It can be incredibly depressing to the unprepared."

It's been a rough day, that's for sure. I don't know if I have the mental fortitude to be surrounded by death every day. I want to try, though. I've never been the type of person who gives up easily, even when stressed.

"*Well?*" Azrael presses me for an answer. "Have you decided to continue, or would you rather go back to regular guidework? Either way, I won't judge you."

It doesn't matter if he'd judge me or not. If I quit this soon, I would judge myself. I would hate to give up before I've really given it a shot.

After a moment of deliberation, I give him a nod. "I would like to continue."

"Good. For now, you are dismissed. I have an unfathomable amount of paperwork that requires my attention." Bowing to me, he adds, "Good day, Miss Alvarez."

"*Wait!*" I grab his sleeve before he can escape. "I... don't know how to warp. Is it too far to walk from Asylum One to my house?"

"Probably." With a sigh and a not-so-subtle roll of his eyes, he warps me to my front door. "There. Practice warping. You'll need it."

I sense he's about to leave, so I stop him again. "Wait... where and when am I supposed to meet you next?"

"I'll contact you on your LightTab. Farewell."

In the blink of an eye, he's gone.

And now I have a *lot* to think about.

Chapter Four

I DESCRIBE MY DAY WITH Azrael in great detail, omitting no part of the story. By the time I finish, my mom is shaking her head.

"Nuh uh. No way!" she objects. "I don't think you should do this, Lucy. You're so young. You don't need to take on any extra stress."

A part of me agrees with her. It *was* stressful. But another part of me is honored that I was chosen to work with an Archangel. Not many students are offered the opportunity.

"It wasn't so bad," I lie—and I know it's a lie because I'm still haunted by the image of baby Isaac in his light bubble. I can't get it out of my head. "I think I can handle it."

"But why? Guidework is fun. Death isn't." When my mom's finger starts wagging, I know she means business. I've seen the wagging finger a lot. It waves like a brandished sword beneath my chin. "Eres estúpido?"

"Mom, why are you making a huge fuss about this? I don't think it's so bad," I argue. "What if I told you I was going to be a doctor? I doubt you'd have a freak-out, and they're surrounded by death too!"

"Doctors save lives. You'll be taking them."

As I consider my mom's opinion, I manifest a box of Reese's Pieces and rip it open. I'm obsessed with Reese's Pieces. When I had cancer, I was in and out of hospitals all the time. When my friends would visit, I would always ask for a box of Reese's Pieces from the hospital vending machine. I got addicted to them. They're probably the reason I have a big butt. I'm skinny all over, but my butt's still huge. If I ever get to a point where I can alter my physical appearance, my butt will be the first thing to go.

"*Lucyyyy,*" Mom whines my name. "Will you think about what I'm saying? I don't want to see you come home in a bad mood everyday."

"I doubt I'll be in a bad mood. Death is sad, but... the Asylum was nice. It's nice to think there's a place for spirit children. I never knew it existed."

An exasperated sigh explodes from Mom's mouth like a bomb. She doesn't want me to forget how much she disapproves. "I'd heard of the Asylums, but I've never stepped foot in one."

Candies rattle around in my mouth as I reply, "Well, it was nice."

I turn on my LightTab and search for the Asylum closest to me. According to the statistic I read, there are over two hundred Asylums, but not all of them are in use. The one closest to our house is Asylum Seventeen. If I visited, I wonder if I would be welcome there?

"I think I might check out Asylum Seventeen. Do you want to come with me?" I ask.

"I would, mija, but I have a mission today. A *fun* mission. Grandma and I are trying to find a dog for a young man named Ethan."

That might sound like fun to her, but it sounds tedious to me. I would rather do something meaningful. Maybe Amber recognized that and chose me for a reason?

"Well... you enjoy that. I haven't been contacted by Azrael yet, so I think I'll head to Asylum Seventeen." I store the rest of my candy in my purse and head to the door. "See you later, Mamá."

I try to warp, but I still can't figure it out, so I head down the block on foot. According to the LightTab, Asylum Seventeen is only four blocks away. I know I'm close when I start hearing joyful squeals from the Asylum's residents. Children at play are always loud, no matter where they come from.

There's a playground in front of the Asylum, with swings, seesaws, and even a bouncy castle. If I was a little bit younger, I would be tempted to hop in and bounce around a bit. Sometimes I wonder why I ever wanted to get older. Being a child was fun.

The interior of Asylum Seventeen is a little less fancy than the one I visited yesterday. It doesn't look like a castle, it looks more like a living room, with couches, a tv, and modern art on the walls. This must be come kind of common room. A couple of preteen boys are playing a very competitive video game. When they start swatting each other, I wonder if I should intervene.

A young guy rushes into the room and shouts, "*Hey*! No hitting!"

One of the boys protests, "Hayyan was cheating, though! He stole one of my weapons!"

The young man, who doesn't look much older than me, says, "That's still no reason to hit him. Please control yourselves, or you'll lose your game privileges for the day."

The boys accept their superior's edict with simultaneous sighs and go back to playing their game.

When the guy finally notices me, I give him a smile. He's kind of cute. He has curly blond hair, a smattering of freckles on his nose, and puppy-like eyes. If he's not an angel, he should be. He has the right look.

"Who are you?" he asks. "If you're not one of the volunteers, you have to schedule an appointment to come here."

"Sorry..." The tone of his voice has me feeling somewhat sheepish. "I, uh... I'm actually one of Azrael's Helpers. Well... I'm training to be a Helper. I just started yesterday."

"In that case, you're welcome to stay." One of his hands shoots out as he approaches, so I give it a reluctant shake. "I'm Sam."

"I'm Lucy." Glancing at the boys, I ask, "So... do you work here?"

"I do. I'm one of the volunteers," Sam says. "I teach math and take care of the babies sometimes."

Maybe I shouldn't bash the subject he teaches, but my disgust flies out of my mouth. "Eww. Math."

Chuckling, Sam says, "You'd be surprised by how often I get that reply."

"That wouldn't surprise me. I can't understand why anyone would like math. My brother did, but... yuck." I'm worried I might be making a bad impression, so I change the subject. "You, uh... have you worked here long?"

"For a couple of decades. I had to wait until I reached angel status. Before that, I lived here myself."

My eyebrows jump at his reply. "Really?"

"Yeah. I was an Asylum kid," he answers with a smile. "I really liked living here, though. I made a lot of friends. I learned a lot. I enjoy being a volunteer too. It's fulfilling work."

I only catch half of what he says because I'm distracted by the light on his curly blonde hair. I don't think I've ever seen such luminous hair.

Sam asks, "So... you're one of Azrael's Helpers?"

"No, I'm a Helper-in-training," I correct him. "If I'm not supposed to be here, you're welcome to kick me out."

"No, you can stay. I'd have to be an idiot to kick you out." When his smile grows, the most adorable dimples appear on his cheeks. "Why would I ask a pretty girl to leave? That would be stupid."

Pretty girl. Sam's compliment echoes in my head until I feel a bit giddy. I've never been told I'm pretty by anyone who wasn't my mom. My childhood bully used to call me *sick girl*, not *pretty girl*. A compliment is a nice change.

I suddenly want to know more about this guy, so I ask, "Where are you from? You know... when you were alive." He has an interesting accent, but I can't quite place it.

"Cape Town, South Africa," he replies. "I died when I was twelve."

"That's so young." I don't know why my reply is even necessary, since *everyone* in the Asylum died young.

"True. And my parents didn't die until forty years later. For the longest time, the Asylum was all I knew." When Hayyan and the other boy start smacking each other with their controllers, he gives them another cautionary, "*Hey!*"

I want to ask more questions, but I've never been good with small talk, especially when the guy is cute. I should be glad I'm not a stuttering mess.

As soon as the boys have settled down, Sam asks, "Lucy, would you like to stay for snack time? Only a few of the kids can manifest, so I usually gather them up for a snack every now and then. Today's snack is pizza."

I don't have a chance to answer. Azrael's voice, deep and deadpan, interrupts, "She can't. We have another mission to attend."

When I turn around, the Angel of Death is standing right behind me. It was freaky to hear his voice all of a sudden. He could have said *hello* first.

Sam says, "That's a shame. Well... maybe another time?"

I give him a nod, but Azrael doesn't give us a chance to iron out any plans. He warps us to our next mission—and presumably another death.

Chapter Five

CLAIRE HAWKINS. 76 years old. Stay-at-home mother of three, grandmother of eight. She is suffering from stage four cancer that has spread throughout her body.

I'm the kind of girl who smiles a lot, but I can feel the corners of my mouth slipping as I read about our new charge. I'm no stranger to cancer, and even though Claire's a lot older than me, I can sympathize with her. Cancer sucks.

Claire is in hospice, where she currently has a visitor. She's sitting up in bed, looking a bit dazed, likely from the medicines they've pumped into her. Her hair and brows were lost to her cancer treatments, so she has a scarf wrapped around her head.

A forty-something guy, probably her son, is readjusting her pillow. "Hey, Mom... I have some good news for you," he says. "I got engaged yesterday."

"To be married?" Claire gasps, and with some effort, she raises her hand to her heart. "I thought it would never happen!"

Her son chuckles at her reaction. "Yeah. Me neither."

I glance at Azrael, who seems to have gone into one of his meditative states. I wonder what he's thinking when he gets like that. Is he thinking anything at all?

Claire asks, "So, who's the lucky lady?"

"It's Florence, Mom. You remember her, don't you? You've met her several times."

"Is she the black girl?"

The son answers with a sigh, "Yeah."

"Oh, good. I liked her. I always thought she was good for you. It's a shame I won't live to see the wedding."

"You don't know that for sure," the son protests.

"Oh, yes I do!" Claire insists. "Unless you were planning on getting married tomorrow?"

The next time I glance at Azrael, his eyes are open, but they focus on nothing. Sullenly, he tells me, "She'll be dead tomorrow."

"Do you know that for a fact?" I ask, but I don't get an answer. I probably shouldn't question him. Someone called the *Angel of Death* probably knows what he's talking about.

"Bring Florence the next time you visit, Philip... if you don't think she'd mind. I'd like to see her again," Claire requests. If Azrael's right, there's a good chance she's seen the last of Florence.

A few minutes after we arrive, more visitors flood into Claire's room. It's a woman, about fifty, with two teen boys and a preteen girl.

When they enter, Claire declares, "Oh, look. It's the baby of the family!"

"Mom... I'm not the baby. Jenny's the baby," the woman corrects her. "I know we look alike, but we're fifteen years apart."

I'm about to ask Azrael if she's suffering from some kind of dementia, but Claire surprises me. For a dying woman, she's pretty sharp.

"I wasn't talking about you, I was talking about Sophia!" Claire pats her bed, motioning for her grandchildren to come forward. "Sophia, come sit with me. I want to see your pretty face up close."

Sophia does better than that. She runs to her grandmother's bed and throws her arms around her.

"I love you, Grandma Claire!" the little girl cries. "I love you! I love you, *please* don't die!"

Claire rips a tissue from the nearby Kleenex box and presses it into her granddaughter's hand. The tissue's ineffective, though. Sophia soaks her grandma's shoulder in tears.

"Don't cry, honey. Grandma will be alright," Claire says. "I won't be in any pain anymore, and I can watch over you in heaven."

If only she knew how true that was. Wiping tears from my eyes, I turn toward Azrael. I don't know how he manages to look so calm and collected during such a heartbreaking scene. Maybe it's an acquired skill?

I don't know if I'd want to acquire that skill, though. I prefer to be warm, not cold.

Claire strokes her granddaughter's hair and whispers, "Grandma loves you, Sophia. You know that, right?"

Sophia answers with a nod and a sniffle, "Yeah."

"You were always my favorite... always my favorite little girl." Grandma kisses Sophia's head at least a half-dozen times before she releases her from their hug. "Never forget me, okay?"

"Never!" Sophia declares. She's finally using the tissue to sop up some of her tears.

For a moment, my eyes get stuck on Claire's hands. They're bony and tremulous, and covered in paper-thin skin. Every time she lifts a hand to touch her granddaughter's hair, it's a labor of love. She can barely move.

I suddenly ask Azrael, "Why don't Archangels grant more miracles?"

He casts a sidelong glance in my direction. "Life itself is a miracle. Every moment is a miracle. Every bond is a miracle. Claire embracing her granddaughter one last time is a miracle to me."

"That's a crappy answer," I tell him. "You know what I mean... a *real* miracle. Would it really be so difficult to help Claire? I know you could make it happen. Stage four cancer would be nothing for an Archangel. Why don't you help more often?"

"Miss Alvarez, Claire is an old woman. She—"

I interrupt, "She's not *that* old."

"She is at the end of her journey, and about to begin a new one," Azrael says. "You now know the afterlife isn't so bad."

"But... look how many people she's leaving behind!" I point at the teenage boys who are inching closer to their grandma's bed. They mumble a few words of sympathy before doling out one-armed hugs.

"She will lose *and* she will gain," Azrael says. "Tomorrow, you will understand."

Azrael has a tendency to be aggravatingly cryptic. I wish he'd give me more straightforward answers.

Claire's visitors stay for a little over an hour, and one by one, they leave. Sophia cries again as she embraces her grandma one last time. Of course, she has no way of knowing it will be their final hug. According to Azrael, it will be.

When her family is out of the room, one of the hospice nurses comes in to administer morphine and tuck Claire into bed. Every time I had morphine, I would always get tired, so she'll probably be asleep soon enough.

"Since we're here, we should try to grant her last wish," Azrael suggests. "I know you're no longer a spirit school student, but you should probably practice with your crystal."

"Okay." I take out my quartz crystal and grip it in my hand. After a moment of concentration, Claire's thoughts flood into my head.

I wish the tv was on. I can't quite reach the remote. I wish I could rewatch my favorite episodes of I Love Lucy... just one last time.

I assume Azrael can hear her thoughts too, so I don't waste time talking about it. I just come up with a plan. "I'll try to get one of the nurses in here. When they come, encourage Claire to ask about the remote."

Azrael gives me an approving nod, so I put my plan into action. I feel like a novice who's pretending to be a veteran, but I hope that's not the impression I give to Azrael. I want him to think I know what I'm doing.

I leave the room, locate one of the nurses, and convince her to return to Claire's room. As soon as she enters, Claire says, "Good... you're here! Can you find the remote for me?"

Obviously, Azrael had no problem getting through to Claire. When I give him a wink, he doesn't flinch or smile or anything. *Predictable.*

The nurse locates the remote near Claire's feet, well out of her reach. As soon as they turn on the tv, a black and white episode of *I Love Lucy* is the first thing they land on. I'm too young to know what the show is about, but Lucy's still recognizable to me.

"Oh my god!" Gasping, I turn to Azrael. "It's the right show and everything! How did you do that?"

Azrael doesn't divulge his secret, but this time, *he* winks at *me*.

Chapter Six

TWO DAYS LATER, CLAIRE is still hanging on. I guess even the Angel of Death doesn't know everything, because she's outlasted his prediction. Still, it's only a matter of time, because she's unconscious now, and many of her organs are shutting down.

Azrael and I come back to check on her every now and then. Even though she's not responsive anymore, she still has visitors. We finally see her second daughter, Jenny, two days after the others visited. Jenny sits near the bed, rests her head on Claire's stomach, and cries as quietly as she can.

"I love you, Mom," says a very nasal Jenny, who kisses her mother's hand, then dries her eyes with a tissue. "I love you. You were the best mom in the world. We were lucky to have you. You'll..." Jenny breaks down crying, so it takes her a moment to finish her thought. "You'll be with Dad soon."

"This is true," Azrael says. He's sitting next to me, his long legs crossed. "I have to get in contact with Henry Hawkins soon."

"That's her husband?" I ask.

Azrael gives me a nod and goes back to reading on his LightTab. Unlike me, he doesn't seem interested in Jenny's breakdown.

Jenny sits with her mom for over an hour, kisses her forehead, and eventually says goodbye.

I don't blame Jenny for leaving. There's something really morbid about sitting around and waiting for someone to die. In fact, it's probably one of the worst ways to spend your time. It makes me think—do I really want to become one of Azrael's Helpers? Do I really want to commit to *this*?

It's late in the evening, so Claire's visitors eventually stop coming. I'm feeling a bit bored, so I manifest a box of Reese's Pieces, kick off my shoes, and indulge myself in bits of peanutty heaven.

"What are those?"

Azrael's question makes me sit up in my chair. "Are you serious? You've never had Reese's Pieces before?"

"No. Is that outlandish?"

"Uh... *yeah!*" I exclaim. "Haven't you been around for thousands of years? How have you never had Reese's Pieces before?"

"Are they new?" he asks.

"No!" I grab his hand, uncurl his fingers, and shake a half-dozen candies into his hand. "You've been missing out."

Azrael glares at the bits of candy in his hand. "Are they really that good?"

"Uh... yeah!" There's a *duh* implied by the tone of my voice. "Haven't you seen the ET movie? Dude, the alien in that movie is obsessed with these too."

I guess I've gotten more comfortable with Azrael if I'm calling him *dude*.

"I have never seen that movie," Azrael flatly states. "I'm not a big fan of movies, truth be told. There are many more productive activities that require my attention. Movies are oftentimes a mindless diversion."

"Nuh uh!" I object. "You can learn a lot from movies. When I was sick, I used to watch movies all day long. Besides... you should try to balance work and play. Don't you ever stop working?"

"Not really."

I almost burst out laughing when Azrael nibbles one of the Reese's Pieces. He's barely biting on the edge of the shell. "You know what I think? It sounds like Archangel Azrael needs to take some time for himself!"

I pop a few candies in my mouth, hoping he'll learn the proper way to eat these.

"I can't just ignore my work to binge movies," Azrael says.

"Sure you can. That's why you have Helpers. You can leave your work to them and fire up a copy of The Avengers."

He matter-of-factly states, "I'm not familiar with that movie."

"Okay, what movies *have* you seen?" When he doesn't answer, I test him with some of the most popular movies of all time. "Wizard of Oz?"

"No."

"*Are you serious?*" My voice is shrill with disbelief. "What abouuuut... The Shawshank Redemption?"

He shakes his head.

"*Star Wars?*"

"I have seen parts of that movie."

"There are a bunch of Star Wars movies. Which one did you see?" He can't answer, so I doubt he's seen much at all. "Azrael... when we have some downtime between missions, I'm going to make you watch a movie with me!"

Azrael responds to my declaration with a sigh, finishes his Reese's Pieces, and swipes a screen on his LightTab. I guess he's officially done with this conversation, but I'm not.

"I'll look at a list of the Top 100 movies of all time and pick one," I tell him. "Did you like your Reese's Pieces?"

"They were fine. Now... back to work. I just contacted Henry Hawkins, Betty Grace and Peter Grace on my LightTab, because Claire is going to die at any minute. If you have any respect for her at all, you'll stop talking about candy and movies."

My expression turns sour when he chastises me. I don't think I was being disrespectful.

One by one, three spirits warp into the room. They identify themselves as Claire's husband, mother and father. As they greet me with handshakes, I shoot a glare at Azrael. I don't think he realized how much he hurt my feelings with his last remark. It was cruel for him to suggest I have no respect for Claire.

Soon after Claire's family arrives, our vigil ends. All of a sudden, she's standing outside of her body, staring at the shell she left behind.

"Oh dear..." Claire whispers. "I think I died!"

Azrael speaks first, capturing her attention, "Indeed you did, Mrs. Hawkins. I assume my companions need no introduction?"

When she has her first glimpse of the family she's missed, Claire squeaks with joy. She crashes into her husband's open arms with such force, she almost knocks him over.

"You look so young!" Claire exclaims. "You *all* look so young. Am I still old?"

"You look beautiful, dear," Henry assures her. "You're every bit as beautiful as the day I met you."

Claire steps out of her husband's embrace and swats his arm. "Don't lie to me, Henry Hawkins! I haven't seen you in eight years, but I can still tell when you're lying."

She hugs her parents next. When her mother's arms wrap around her, Claire loses composure and wails behind her shuddering hands.

"I never stopped missing you, Mom, Dad..." Claire says. "I never thought I'd see you again!"

"Well, we've *always* been with you," her mom says. "But it's been a long time since I've hugged my little girl, so it's an exciting day for me as well."

It's kind of funny to hear her say *little girl* when Claire looks older than all of them. I wonder what it will be like when I see my brother and father again? What if my brother, Luis, outlives me by sixty years? That could potentially be a strange union. If he lives that long, he might not even care to see me again.

Azrael explains the situation to Claire: he's taking her *Home*, where she will reside with the spirit members of her family. Claire looks excited by the prospect, but I'm sure she's sad to leave her children and grandchildren behind. That's how I felt. I was happy to be with Mom, but I didn't want to leave Dad and Luis. I was torn.

When we get Home, Claire asks Azrael, "Who are you? And who is that pretty young lady?"

"I'm Archangel Azrael." Bowing his head in my direction, he answers on my behalf, "And this is Lucy, one of my Helpers."

Wow. He's already introducing me as one of his Helpers? I didn't expect that.

I guess I can't back out now.

Chapter Seven

I GET A TEXT FROM AZRAEL, informing me there will be no mission today. Now that I've got some free time, I think I'll try to make some new friends.

I return to Asylum Seventeen and search for Sam. When I find him, he's rocking one of the babies in his arms. My heart melts as soon as I see him. I don't think there's anything more adorable than a guy taking care of a baby.

When he spots me, he cries, "Lucy! You're back! I'm glad. I was afraid I wouldn't see you again."

"We'll have to sync up our LightTabs so we can text," I suggest. "Are you busy? If you are, I can come back later."

"No, please. Stay. I more or less make my own schedule around here." Sam kisses the baby's head before lowering her to her crib. The gesture is so sweet, I could cry. "Hey, why don't I round up the kids for snack time? The last time you were here, Azrael took you away."

"I'd really like that." When he leaves the nursery, I stick to him like a shadow. "So... what's today's snack?"

"Your choice," Sam says.

I almost choose Reese's Pieces, but I realize not everyone is obsessed with peanut butter in a crispy shell. I should probably choose something that everyone can enjoy—maybe something that's more like a meal? "How about tacos?" I suggest.

"That's a really good idea!" Sam exclaims. "I'll manifest a bowl of cheese, tomatoes, lettuce... the kids can make them however they'd like. That'd probably be fun for them."

A dreamy sigh accidentally slips out of me as I listen to him. I don't know if it's his South African accent, his blonde hair, or the fact that he works with children, but something about him gives me a fluttery feeling in my heart.

I help Sam with our "taco table," where all the essential ingredients are assembled. While Sam leaves to fetch the kids, I grab one of the shells and stuff it with all the delicious goodness it can hold. The cheese is overflowing and taco sauce is dripping down the side. If you ask me, that's the *only* way to make a taco.

Sam escorts about ten kids into the room and lets them make their tacos first. As I munch on my food, I feel a bit guilty. Should I have let the kids go first? Was I wrong to help myself? When taco sauce slides down my chin, I manifest a napkin and wipe it away before Sam can see what a slob I am.

Sam finally gets his tacos and joins me on a couch. By that time, my own taco is long gone.

Between bites, he suggests, "We should do something outside of the Asylum sometime. Don't get me wrong, I love the kids, but they require a lot of attention. It'd be nice to get to know you in another environment."

Maybe I'm reading too much into it, but it almost sounds like he's asking me on a date.

"I'd like that. I haven't really made any friends since I've been here." My answer makes me wince. I hope he doesn't think I've put him in the friend zone.

"Maybe we could go somewhere for lunch?" he suggests. "Does Azrael ever give you a day off?"

"Yeah. I'm off today."

"Good. Maybe we can get together on your next off day?"

I wanted to do something *today*, but I don't think he took the hint. I give him a nod and keep my disappointment to myself.

Sam says, "Tacos was a good idea. The kids seem to like them."

"*Of course* they like them. I have literally never met anyone who didn't like tacos."

"They have a math lesson after this. Would you like to stay for that?"

Sam winked when he said that, so I think he's being sarcastic. He knows I hate math. "Oh, yeah. That sounds delightful. Sign me up for that."

It suddenly dawns on me that I keep pestering him at his workplace. The next time I see him, we definitely need to get together away from the Asylum. I don't want to make a nuisance of myself, so as soon as taco time is over, I say goodbye.

I still have a lot of time to kill, so I decide to practice warping. I try to warp to my dad's house. *I can't.* I try to warp to Machu Picchu. *I don't go anywhere.* I try to warp to Azrael's location, and suddenly I'm standing in front of Archangel Tower. I appear in front of a guard, who gives me a scathing look when I arrive.

"Can I help you with something, Miss?" he asks.

"Um... is Azrael in there?"

"Who's asking?"

The guard doesn't sound particularly polite, and the spear in his hand is crackling with electricity. If his goal is to intimidate everyone who comes here, he's definitely succeeding.

"I, uh... I'm Lucy Alvarez," I introduce myself. "I'm one of Azrael's Helpers."

"Is he expecting you?"

"Um... n-no, not really." I take a step backward, away from the surly guard. "I'm sorry. I shouldn't have come here. I'll just... go."

I'm about ready to flee when I get a message on my LightTab. It's from Azrael.

Show this to the guard. Tell him to let you in.

Grimacing, I present the LightTab's screen to the guard. I have no idea how Azrael knows I'm here, or why he's helping me, but it's better than walking away with my tail between my legs.

"Alright. Go in." The guard steps aside, but he doesn't look happy about it. This guy looks so unpleasant, I wonder if he's ever happy about anything.

I hurry into Archangel Tower before the guard changes his mind. Now that I'm inside, I have no idea where to go, so I end up wandering the hallways, clueless and awed. I stop to look at a mural of Archangel Michael in some kind of puffy thong. That's more of him than I *ever* thought I'd see.

When the man in the mural suddenly appears beside me, I almost scream. Does Michael know I was just gawking at his nearly-naked body?

"Are you looking for Azrael?" Michael speaks so loudly, his voice echoes down the hall.

I manage to squeak out an answer. "Yes."

"Head up the stairs over there." He points behind me. "Turn to the right, and Azrael's office will be the first door you see."

"Uh... thanks." I steal one last glimpse of the thong mural before I speed away from him.

I follow Michael's directions to Azrael's office. As soon as I tap on the door, I hear, "Come in, Miss Alvarez."

When I enter, Azrael's at his desk, and Archangel Jophiel is studying me with crossed arms. I don't think I'd recognize all of the Archangels, but Jophiel got pretty famous after his trial awhile back.

Jophiel speaks first. "I'm a one-woman man now, but... wow, she's beautiful. I can see why you wanted her to be one of your Helpers."

Beautiful? Wow. I'm pretty sure I'm blushing now. I'm getting way more compliments in the afterlife than I ever got when I was alive.

"I didn't," Azrael replies. "Amber chose her."

"Well, you should send Amber a thank you note. She chose well for you." Jophiel crosses the room and stands right in front of me. "It's lovely to meet you, Miss Alvarez. Don't be fooled by Azrael's giant sword and sour faces. He's actually one of the friendliest Archangels among us."

I don't know how to respond to that, so I just say, "It's nice to meet you too."

Jophiel shuffles past me, and as he exits the room, I hear him murmur, *"He was a bit of an ass for arresting me, but... I forgive him."*

He closes the door behind him, leaving me alone with Azrael. He and I are alone on missions all the time, but for some reason, I feel nervous.

"Why are you here, Miss Alvarez?" Azrael asks.

"Because you let me in?"

When his eyes narrow, I'm already doubting Jophiel's "friendly Archangel" claim.

"I was teaching myself how to warp," I explain. "I tried to warp to your location, and I found myself in front of Archangel Tower. I was going to leave, but I got a message from you on my LightTab, so... I thought you wanted to see me?"

"I thought you were coming here for a purpose," Azrael says. "Nevertheless, congratulations on a successful warp."

"Thanks." I collapse into a plush chair, even though he hasn't invited me to sit. "So... are you busy?"

"I am *always* busy."

"Do you have time to watch a movie?" That's probably a stupid question. There's no way he would want to watch a movie with—

"Sure," Azrael's reply interrupts my thoughts. "Why not?"

His answer stuns me, but not for long. I excitedly manifest a television and a copy of Spielberg's ET. Then I manifest a box of Reese's Pieces because you *can't* watch this movie without Reese's Pieces.

When the movie starts, Azrael notes, "You look happy."

"Of course I am!" I exclaim. "I never expected you to say yes to watching a movie, since you think they're a waste of time, and you're so busy and all."

"Perhaps I said yes to spending time with *you*, Miss Alvarez."

My mind can barely process his reply. Does he actually like spending time with me? I never would have guessed.

I wish he would sit closer to me, but he's still at his desk, looking prim and proper. When we get our first glimpse of the movie's titular alien, I ask, "Are aliens real? If anyone would know the answer to that, it's probably you."

Azrael replies, "I do know, and I'm not at liberty to answer that."

"Oooo!" I rub my hands together. "That sounds like there *are* aliens! One day, I'm going to squeeze the answer out of you."

"Good luck with that."

When I'm out of Reese's Pieces, I manifest a plate of mozzarella sticks. I'm really gorging myself today, but that's the best thing about the afterlife. I can stuff my face without worrying about calories.

I'm dead quiet during most of the movie, but when we're about halfway, I ask, "Are you enjoying it?"

His answer is disappointing, as usual. "It's tolerable."

"If you don't like movies... what do you do for fun?" I ask. "Does Archangel Azrael *ever* have fun time?"

"Not really."

I have no idea why I ask my next question. It just flies out of my mouth. "Do you have a girlfriend?"

He pauses a moment, shakes his head, and answers with a sigh, "No. Not for several decades."

"Oh." I almost tell him I've never had a boyfriend, but I doubt he'd be interested. It's not that hard to figure out, though. A week after my fifteenth birthday, I found out I had cancer. After that, finding a boyfriend wasn't too high on my list of priorities.

As soon as the credits start rolling, Azrael says, "Thank you for the diversion, Miss Alvarez. I should really get back to my work now."

"*Was* it diverting?" I ask. "Were you entertained?"

"The ending was... touching."

His answer almost makes me squeal. "I know, right? It's a sob fest. It always makes me cry."

"You are a very exuberant young lady, Miss Alvarez," he says. "Now, will you let me return to my work?"

"Alright, *fine!*" I stick out my tongue at him, but his eyes are on his paperwork, so he doesn't see it. "See you tomorrow?"

"Yes." Azrael echoes me, "See you tomorrow."

Even though he dismissed me a bit rudely, I still smile on my way out. In my head, I'm already plotting.

What movie should we watch next?

Chapter Eight

MOVIES WILL HAVE TO wait for another day, because Azrael and I have another mission. As usual, I have no idea what to expect, so I brace myself for anything. We warp to the middle of a desert, where tumbleweeds are plentiful and life is scarce. If I was affected by temperatures, I'm sure it would be stifling out here.

Glancing around the area, I spot six cacti, a lizard, a horse, and one man. I assume the man is going to be our charge.

"The year is 1882, and that man is indeed our charge," Azrael informs me. "If you want to know the rest, read your LightTab, and listen to his thoughts."

1882, huh? This is only the second time I've been on a mission that didn't feel "modern." Our charge is sitting in a cactus' shade, using his hat to fan himself. His face is dirty, but his forehead is so slick with sweat, some of the filth has rinsed from his skin. He must be dying. After all, why would we be here if he wasn't dying?

As a "Helper," I know what my job is supposed to be, but I'm still surprised when our guy coughs into a rag and the cloth is covered in blood. Coughing blood is never a good sign.

I check my LightTab to learn more about the guy in front of me.

Oliver Robbins is a forty-seven-year-old married father of three. He and his wife, Mary, have been together for almost thirty years. He's a former ranch hand and gambling addict. Over the last year, his tuberculosis has been getting significantly worse.

"The disease will claim him soon," Azrael fills in the blanks for me. "He's in the final stages. It's only a matter of time. Have you heard his thoughts yet?"

"No. Give me a moment." How fast does he expect me to do this? He needs to understand I'm still a novice, barely out of school. Sighing, I pull out my quartz crystal and focus my attention on Oliver. I'm sure Azrael can hear his thoughts a lot clearer than I can. I only catch snippets.

Can't leave them with nothing... deserve better... Mary and the kids... make them rich... to the bank.

"It was sort of... unclear," I confess. "I heard something about a bank?"

"That was the most significant part." Azrael squats next to Oliver and places a hand on his shoulder. "I'm giving him an energy boost. I don't think he'll get back on his feet without one."

"What about a bank?" I ask.

"Oliver's final wish is to rob a bank, to leave his family with money when he passes away. And we're going to help him with that."

"*What?*" I shriek. "Do we have to?"

"Angels and spirits are supposed to assist their charges no matter what, entirely without judgment," Azrael explains. "I will help him. However, if your morals won't allow it, you don't have to help. You're welcome to take a loss instead. Many spirits do."

"Stealing is wrong. *Wrong*," I insist. This is the first time I've been tasked with a questionable mission. "Why would I want to help someone commit a crime?"

"You might want to ask yourself if he's doing the wrong thing for the right reasons," Azrael suggests. "He's a desperate man, close to death, who wants to help his family. As morally questionable as it is, I can understand him."

"I don't know. Maybe..." Is it alright to disagree with an Archangel? I might tag along, but I don't know how actively I want to participate.

A few seconds after receiving Azrael's energy boost, Oliver is back on his feet and ready for action. When he whistles for his horse, the nickering black stallion trots to his side.

"His destination is a town called Oakley," Azrael says. "Either we can warp there and wait for him to arrive... or we can fly there. It's your choice."

I don't have wings of my own, so if we flew there, he'd have to carry me. Azrael would have to put his arms around me, and I would rather spare myself the awkwardness of that. "Let's warp there," I vote.

Azrael must be satisfied by that answer, because he takes my arm and warps us to Oakley. A big, wooden BANK sign is directly above our heads.

I warn my instructor, "If Oliver starts shooting people, I'm out! I barely want to help a robber. I *definitely* don't want to help a murderer!"

Azrael answers coolly, "That's perfectly understandable, Miss Alvarez."

Since I've been a spirit, I've had some pretty crazy days, but this is the wildest of all. I'm in the Old West, surrounded by horse-drawn buggies and buildings that look like a movie set. Ladies in fine dresses and men in ten-gallon hats are ambling along the boardwalk, oblivious to the robbery that will soon take place.

I ask Azrael, "Has a spirit ever tried to sabotage their mission?"

"It's been known to happen."

"I'm not thinking about sabotage myself... I'm just curious." I have nothing to do while I wait, so I manifest a cowboy hat and stick it on Azrael's head.

"What are you doing?" he asks, in a voice as dull as ever.

"I thought you needed a hat," I tell him. "Do you think I need a hat? Or do you..."

As soon as I see Oliver approaching on his horse, my mind drops its thought. He got here much sooner than I expected. He dismounts his horse, ties it to a hitching post, and pulls his scarf over his nose, concealing his face.

When Oliver reaches for his gun, Azrael whispers to me, "This is it. Get ready."

Oliver raises his pistol, storms into the bank, and tosses an empty sack on the counter. "Fill that up!" he demands. "And fill it up quick! I ain't got all day."

I hear a squeal from a lady in the bank, and two men are trying to sink behind the counter, out of view. One of the bankers tries to reach under the counter for his rifle. Azrael sends the rifle flying away, out of the man's grasp.

I hiss at my instructor, "I can't believe you're helping with this!"

Azrael's head shakes at my disapproval. "This is my job, Miss Alvarez. I'm doing exactly what I'm supposed to do."

"Fill it up!" Oliver demands again. "And don't try to be the hero. I got my eye on you."

Beads of silvery sweat speckle the banker's forehead as he stuffs Oliver's sack with ample stacks of cash. When it's full, Oliver snatches it out of his hand and tucks the big bag under his arm.

"Thank you very much, sir," Oliver says, tipping his hat to the teller. "Now... I'm going to back out of here. Try anything funny, and I won't hesitate to shoot you between the eyes."

I poke Azrael's arm and complain, "We're helping a guy who threatens to shoot people. That's just *great*."

He ignores my concerns and follows Oliver from the building. As soon as he's out, our charge jumps on his horse, pulls down his mask, and gallops from the scene of the crime as fast as his horse can run.

"Now... we follow him," Azrael says. "We need to make sure he makes it to his home. Come."

This time, I don't have a choice. Azrael wraps his arms around me, expands his wings, and takes off after Oliver. He flies fast, keeping a close watch on our mark and his horse.

Flying with Azrael is as weird as I thought it would be. This is exactly the awkwardness I hoped to avoid. My back is crushed against his chest, and his arms are tight around my waist. It's weirdly intimate, and I hope it's over soon.

Something tells me it won't be, because I doubt Oliver would rob a bank that was too close to his home.

A few minutes after we leave Oakley, we hear gunfire and yelps. It looks like someone is after Oliver's money, but I can't tell if it's the law or more bad guys.

Oliver jumps from his horse, takes cover behind a cactus, and readies his gun. As soon as he places me on my feet, Azrael confirms my fears, "They're outlaws. They're trying to rob a thief and take his loot."

"Are you sure?"

"I'm absolutely sure," Azrael says. "I've put up a shield around Oliver. That should prevent any bullets from striking him."

"Okay," I whimper. So far, I've been opposing Oliver and his questionable morals, but now I'm totally on his side. It's three against one, and these guys are scabs who want to feed off of another bandit's work. Where is the honor in that?

To be fair, where is the honor in *any* of this?

"Actually, Miss Alvarez, it's two against one," Azrael corrects me. "One of the men is with his spirit guide, but I should be able to handle that."

Azrael charges at Oliver's opponents, and when he draws his sword, I hear the spirit guide shout, "*Archangel Azrael? Shit!*" As Azrael's sword arcs upward, a bright red shockwave is loosed from the blade. The outlaw's spirit guide is instantly frozen, and his charge is knocked off his feet.

When the bandit sees his buddy go down, he shouts, "James, what the hell is wrong with you? Get your ass up!"

But James doesn't get up. He's pinned to the ground, knocked unconscious by Azrael's massive wave. I'm trying not to be impressed, but I am. Whatever Azrael unleashed was powerful enough to freeze the human *and* his spirit.

Shots are exchanged between Oliver and the remaining outlaw. Bullets pepper our charge's cactus, but he's impervious to damage. While they're shooting at each other, Azrael's sword releases such a powerful wave, it shakes the ground. When the wave hits, the remaining outlaw collapses on his back.

While all this is happening, I'm cowering behind the cactus with Oliver, looking as panicked as he does. I'm close enough to hear him whisper, "What the hell..."

Realizing his enemies are incapacitated, he climbs back on his horse and canters away. Azrael's hat is tilting when he returns to me.

I don't want to congratulate him too much, so I stick to weak praise. "That was... interesting."

"That's one word for it. Now... are you ready to get back to it?"

When his arms slide around my waist again, I groan.

Chapter Nine

OLIVER COUGHS UP MORE blood than ever, and when he slumps over in his saddle, I fear the worst. What if he's dead and never makes it back? I know he's a criminal, but there's a small part of me that wants to see him succeed.

Azrael says, "He's not dead, Miss Alvarez. If he was, you would see him standing near his corpse."

"Oh. Right. Good point," I answer sheepishly.

"Nevertheless, his condition is worsening by the minute. It seems he waited until the last possible moment to commit his crime." Azrael holds onto me with one arm, flies closer to our charge, and gives him another boost of energy. "That should sustain him until he reaches his home."

Reinvigorated, Oliver grabs his horse's reigns and trots forward.

I ask, "How much further does he have to go?" Azrael seems to know everything, so I assume he has an answer.

"Not much further. At his current speed, I expect him to arrive within ten minutes."

"Good." I'll be happy to see him back with his family, and even happier to get out of Azrael's arms.

The Robbins family has a small ranch in the middle of nowhere. They live on the edge of the desert, where grass is too sparse for grazing animals. As we pass over the few cows they have, my heart breaks. The poor animals are in dire need of food.

Oliver is greeted by two of his three children: a girl and a boy. The girl is about twelve, and the boy is a few years younger. As their father dismounts his horse, the boy says, "Molly said you left us for good! She said you were dying but you didn't want to die in front of us, so you left."

The girl—I assume she's Molly—swats her little brother's arm. "I didn't say that! I said *maybe* he left us. I never said it was certain!"

"Aw, I'd never leave you kids!" Oliver ruffles his son's hair and heads to the stable with his horse. "I *am* dying, but—" His thought is interrupted by one of his many coughing fits.

As soon as Azrael sets me on my feet, I put distance between us. For the rest of the day, I intend to keep him at arm's length.

"What's it like to die?" asks the little boy, whose name I have yet to learn.

"I dunno, son. I'm not dead yet."

After spirit school, my LightTab got an upgrade. Now I can use it to scan humans and learn a few random facts about them. I haven't used it yet, so I try it on Oliver's son.

Oliver Robbins, 10. Has a crippling fear of snakes and a bully named Fred.

"Are you in a lot of pain, though?" asks Oliver Jr. "Ma says you're in a lot of pain all the time."

"It's not so bad. It's no worse than having a cough or a cold."

I'm pretty sure that's a lie, but I understand why he's downplaying his pain for little Oliver's sake.

Both Molly and Oliver Jr. follow their father to the barn, where he stables his tired horse. Molly pokes her dad's money sack and asks, "What's this?"

"It's money. A *lot* of money. Don't tell your mom, but..." Oliver slips a few bills from the bag and presents them to his kids.

"This is a whole two dollars!" Oliver Jr. exclaims. "Are you really giving this to us?"

"I sure am. But like I said... let's keep it between us."

"Is Susan getting some money too?" Molly asks. "I'd feel bad if I got money and she didn't."

"I'll try to slip her a few dollars before I give the rest to your Ma," Oliver promises. "Speaking of your Ma... where is she? I took off without telling anybody, so I figured she'd be out here to greet me."

"She's in the kitchen makin' chicken," the little Oliver reports. "She's mad at you, Pa. *Really* mad."

The kids scatter after we follow them into the house, and when Oliver tells his wife about the robbery, she gets a lot madder.

"Oliver James Robbins!" As she shrills his entire name, she pitches a wooden spoon at his head. "What are you thinking? Why would you rob a bank? Don't you have any sense in your head? Has that disease addled your brain?"

Oliver dodges a second hurtling spoon and throws up his hands, as if to surrender. "I'm thinking clearer than I've ever thought in my life, Mary! I wanted to do something for you and the kids before I... y'know."

"And you thought you'd do *this*?" Mary grabs the sack of money and slams it on the kitchen table. "This is dirty money, Oliver! Why would you think I'd want this?"

"We can barely get by as it is! Since I been sick, the ranch has gone to hell, and Olly's not old enough for proper work. The kids and the cows need food. Honey... you *need* this."

"I needed my husband to rob a bank?" Mary growls and shakes her head. "No, what I needed was a damn miracle! I needed you to get better. I need—"

Mary's voice breaks up before she can finish. Her lips shudder as she tries to hold back her tears.

"Honey..." Oliver tucks a lock of hair behind her ear and taps her on the nose. "I think we both know I'm not getting any better. Doc says I should be dead already with all the fluid that's in my lungs. I dragged myself out of bed and walked into that bank because I wanted to give you and the kids a better life. Maybe it wasn't the moral thing to do... but it felt like the right thing to do. I don't want to think of you struggling without me. I don't want to leave this world until I know the kids will have food in their stomachs."

When Oliver opens the sack, his wife gasps at the mounds of money.

"How much is this?" she asks.

"I dunno. But I *do* know it's enough for ya'll to live comfortably," Oliver says. "Maybe it wasn't a good thing to do, but I don't regret it. If I can leave this world knowing you'll be alright... I can die a happier man."

"*Oliver...*" There's a lecture in her voice, but I think her resistance might be cracking.

"It'll be good for you," Oliver says. "For once, you can live like a rich lady. It's what you always deserved... but you got me instead."

"Your love made me feel like a rich lady," Mary says, bumping her hip against his. "And I *do* love you, Oliver Robbins. No matter what, I'll always love you."

Mary is the one who hides the money, so I guess she's come around. While his wife is preoccupied, Oliver pays another visit to his kids, including Susan, who finally gets her two dollars. Susan looks like the oldest, but not by much.

"You kids are my world. You know that, don't you?" Oliver says. "You've made me a very happy man."

They mumble various replies, and a couple of them look like they're holding back tears.

"I love you guys," Oliver says. "I might not always be around, but I can promise you this... there's never been a dad who loved his kids more than I love you."

After professing his love to his children, Oliver heads upstairs to the second floor of his house. He almost doesn't make it. A coughing fit forces a pause in the middle of his climb.

"I feel bad for him," I confess to Azrael. "I know he did a bad thing, but... I still feel bad. Dying sucks."

"Indeed it does, Miss Alvarez," Azrael agrees. "That's why we're needed. We're here to make death a little easier for people."

When Oliver reaches his room, he collapses in bed, coughs, and fusses with the chamber of his gun. When I realize he's reloading it, I raise an eyebrow.

Azrael reveals what I already suspect. "He's going to kill himself. He's finished what he set out to do, and he wants his suffering to end."

I shriek, "*Shouldn't we try to stop him?*"

"I have prevented over a thousand suicides. However, in the case of terminal illness, I let my charge make the choice. In some cases, death can be a much needed release."

"Well, *I* think we should stop him!" I exclaim. "Don't his kids deserve a few extra days with their dad?"

"You can try to stop him, if that's your wish, but I'm not going to interfere." Azrael stands in the doorway. With his arms crossed, he looks like some sort of moody sentinel. "He's already said goodbye... in his own way. He doesn't want his slow death to be the last thing his kids remember."

"So you're actually going to just... let him kill himself?" I ask.

"As I said, you can try to stop him." Azrael bows his head at Oliver, who already has the pistol's barrel pressed against his forehead. "But I'm certain he's already made up his mind."

Rushing to Oliver's bed, I yell, "Don't! Stay for Oliver. Stay for Molly! Stay for—"

He squeezes the trigger before I can finish, and the shot echoes through the house.

When Oliver is out of his body, Azrael casually says, "Greetings. I'm Archangel Azrael... and we're here to take you Home."

Chapter Ten

WHEN SAM INVITES ME out to lunch, I'm tormented by a single question: *Is this supposed to be a date?* I wouldn't mind if it *was* a date, because Sam is super cute, and like me, he's the kind of person who smiles more often than not. In other words, he's the exact opposite of Azrael.

Sam even lets me choose the place, so I pick an upscale Mexican restaurant called *Flores*. It's a bright, airy restaurant, brimming with flowers and exotic greenery. It's almost like dining in a conservatory. It's a little posh, so I wear a dress and high heels. This is the first time I've ever worn high heels, so it takes me awhile to get used to them.

When I was alive, I never would have eaten at a place like this. My family wouldn't have been able to afford it. This is one of the perks of being dead, I guess. Nobody has to worry about money anymore.

Sam's sitting across from me, looking adorable in his fuzzy blue sweater. Every time he talks, his accent melts my ears.

"So, how do you like being one of Azrael's Helpers?"

"It's, um..." How do I describe my experience without sounding like I completely hate it? "It's been... trying."

"I can imagine," Sam says. "Aren't you always watching someone die?"

"Pretty much." As I'm browsing the culinary options, Archangel Azrael walks into Flores. I hold the menu over my face, hiding from view.

Can I not catch a break? Of all the restaurants he could have picked, Azrael just happens to choose *this one*? This is way beyond coincidence. For some reason, my instructor wants to spy on me.

While I'm peeking at Azrael over the top of my menu, Sam asks, "What do you think is the hardest part of the job?"

"My first job was definitely the hardest," I tell him. "The idea of taking a baby from their mother is just heartbreaking."

"True. But... at least they'll be reunited someday, right? You can take some solace in that."

I'm only half-listening to Sam because my eyes are locked on Azrael. *Is* he spying on me? If I keep watching him, am *I* technically spying on *him*? He's all alone, which surprises me. For a split second, I consider inviting him to our table, but if this really *is* a date, I don't want to spoil it.

"Most of my friends think I'm crazy, but... I like working with the children," Sam says. "It's really fulfilling work. If Azrael doesn't accept you on his team, you could always come work with me. I think you'd be good at it."

"Umm... wh-why don't you think he'd accept me for his team?" As I stutter the question, my menu creeps higher, blocking my entire face. Azrael just glanced in this direction, and I don't want him to see me.

"Archangel Azrael is notoriously strict. He turns away almost half of the spirits who undergo his training."

"Really? That's the first time I've heard that." When the waitress comes, I order something called a quesadilla burrito. Unfortunately, I have to surrender my menu, so I can no longer use it as a shield. Azrael's attention is on his LightTab, so I'm safe for now.

Why am I trying to hide from him? Am I worried about him seeing me with another guy? If so, *why* am I worried? It makes no sense.

"I don't think you have anything to worry about, though. You seem like a girl who would be dedicated to any job, and I'm sure Azrael will see that too." After a short pause, Sam gives me another compliment. "Your hair is a beautiful color, by the way."

"What? Really?" I gather my hair onto a single shoulder and observe its color with a sneer. "It looks pretty ordinary to me."

"No, it's really pretty. It's like chocolate brown, but with traces of auburn. It's lovely."

As he describes the color, a smile raises my lips. I would have described it as *dull brown*, but I like his interpretation much better.

When there's a lull in the conversation, I take out my LightTab. I start to send a text to Azrael, to ask why he's here, but I decide against it. As I stare at his name and the blank message on my screen, I have a strange revelation. *Azrael* and *Alvarez* are almost an anagram. All I have is an extra *V*. I wonder if that's significant in some way?

"What are you looking at?"

As soon as Sam asks that, I turn off my LightTab and shove it into my bag. "Nothing important. So... you're an angel? Tell me about that."

While Sam talks about the many missions and trials he's faced, my gaze floats back to Azrael. Three pretty girls have amassed around his table. I guess they must be fans, because he stands up and takes pictures with them. For some reason, it's weird to think Azrael has fans.

"There was one mission I had..." Sam chatters, "I had to help a guy steal his brother's girlfriend. At the same time, the brother's spirit guide was my best friend! It turned into a weird competition, with both of us trying to convince the girl who she wanted. In the end, my charge was the victor, but... a part of me always felt bad about that, because it ruined the brothers' friendship."

More girls are surrounding Azrael's table now. He looks grumpy, but he's surprisingly patient with them. He takes a picture with every single girl, and a few of them bombard him with unexpected hugs.

When Azrael's eyes suddenly meet mine, my gaze snaps back to Sam.

"What do you think?" he asks. "Should I feel bad about that?"

I was only listening with half an ear, but I gathered enough to give him a decent reply. "Sometimes, humans ask for strange things. It's not your fault if the guy wanted his brother's girlfriend."

"Yeah, I suppose you're right." Sam accepts my answer with a hitched shoulder. "To be an angel, you have to complete a *lot* of missions. Believe it or not, I still remember every single one of them."

I reply, "I'll probably remember mine forever. They tend to make an impact."

My quesadilla burrito arrives, and it's even better than I expected. I guess I shouldn't be surprised. We're in heaven—or something like it. Everything is perfect here.

At the end of my maybe-date, I send one last glance in Azrael's direction, and he sends one in mine.

If I can, I'm going to forget this awkwardness ever happened.

Chapter Eleven

MY MOM YELLS FROM ANOTHER room, "*Lucy, there's someone here to see you!*"

I don't know a lot of people, so I expect to see Sam, Azrael or Larry, my former instructor. However, my visitor is none of the above. It's a middle-aged black woman with curly burgundy hair and a huge smile on her face.

"Luciana Alvarez? I'm Nikita Samuels, one of Azrael's Helpers. He wants you to be present at today's reunion."

I know I'm going to sound like an idiot, but I have no idea what she's talking about. "Reunion?"

"He didn't tell you about it?" When I shake my head, she explains, "A former resident of Asylum One is going to be reunited with his mother today. His name's Alexander. His mother, Marjorie, gave birth to him more than twenty-five years ago. Sudden infant death syndrome took his life when he was only two months old, and Alexander's been with us ever since."

I hope she's not offended by this question, but I have to ask, "Why didn't Azrael tell me about this? Is he mad at me?"

"No, honey, he's busy," Nikita says. "He's with Marjorie right now. She was in a terrible car accident, and... well... it looks like she's not going to make it. While he's busy with Marjorie, he wants us to pick up Alexander and take him to Asylum One."

In the corner of my eye, I can see my mom shaking her head. She's never approved of my decision to become one of Azrael's Helpers. She still thinks it's causing me too much stress—and she might be right. I'm constantly thinking about death now.

I don't know why Mom would be grouchy about this, though. Reuniting a son and mother sounds like a nice thing.

Nikita warps us to random door of a random apartment building. I assume this is where Alexander lives.

Nikita says, "Before I knock, is there anything you'd like to ask me?"

I'm glad she asked, because I do have a few questions. "Did Marjorie have any other children?"

"No. Sadly, after they lost baby Alexander, Marjorie and her husband split up, and she never got remarried. She's sixty-two now. She lost Alexander when she was in her thirties."

"Thanks for filling me in. This is really helpful," I tell her. Despite the grim subject matter—death, car accidents and lost babies—Nikita manages to sound cheerful. I like working with Azrael, but I think it'd be nice working with Nikita too.

"Any more questions, honey?" she asks.

"No, I think I'm good." I had an aunt who used to call me *honey*. When Aunt Marta said it, it always sounded condescending. When Nikita says it, it sounds sweet.

Nikita knocks on Alexander's door. I've been trying to figure out his age based on the information I've been given. I expect to see a guy who's twenty-five or thirty, but the boy who answers the door looks a few years younger than me. He's no older than fifteen or sixteen, and he has the same cherubic blonde curls that Sam has. I guess I shouldn't be surprised by his youth. Didn't Azrael say something about children choosing to look like children for their parents' sake?

"Hello," Alexander greets us with a weak smile. "Is it time?"

"Yes, I'm afraid it is," Nikita says. "You don't have to worry about your mom, though. She's not in any pain right not. Azrael's made sure of that."

"That's good." Glancing at me, Alexander asks, "Who's this?"

"This is Luciana, one of Azrael's Helpers."

"I'm more like trainee Helper," I say. "This is the first time I've been to a reunion. How do you feel about it?"

Before I get my reply, Nikita warps us to the interior of Asylum One.

"I feel kind of sad... but happy at the same time. It's kind of confusing," answers a shrugging Alexander. "I want to be with my mom, but I also don't want her to die."

"That makes sense. I'd probably be conflicted too."

"I see her all the time. Almost every day," Alexander says. "But this is the first time she'll see me. I'm kind of nervous."

Nikita says, "Well, you look handsome. I'm sure she'll be impressed and proud."

"What do you guys think I should wear?" Alexander asks. "A suit and tie? Or... is that too much? Should I just be casual?"

His current shirt of choice is a graphic tee with a skull on it, so I give him a bit of friendly advice. "Maybe *don't* wear that? I think something like a sweater would be nice."

Alexander takes my suggestion and manifests a pair of khaki pants and a ribbed red sweater. I give my approval with a thumbs up.

"What about my hair? Does it look alright?" Despite positive feedback from both Nikita and me, Alexander manifests a mirror and checks it himself.

"You look *fine*," I assure him. "Like Nikita said, I'm sure your mom will like what she sees."

A few of the Asylum One children trickle into the room to watch the upcoming reunion. I can't blame them for being curious. One day, they'll be in Alexander's shoes.

After about ten minutes, Azrael arrives with Marjorie and another old woman. Nikita identifies her in a whisper, "Marjorie's mother."

Marjorie lets out a sharp cry when she sees her son for the first time. In her sobbing, I can hear her joy, relief and euphoria.

"Ohhh, it's my baby! It's Alexander!" Marjorie runs to him, arms outstretched, and grasps both sides of his head. Caressing his cheeks, she whimpers, "My boy, my boy... oh, look at you! You're so beautiful!"

Alexander responds to her affection with an adorably awkward, "Hi, Mom."

"*Mom!*" Marjorie repeats the word with a shrill. "I've always wanted to hear someone call me that!"

"I call you that *all the time,*" Alexander says. "The only difference is... you can actually hear me now."

Unchecked tears spill down Marjorie's cheeks as she admires the face of her long lost son. Her hands tremble as she fusses with his hair. "It's so curly!" she exclaims. "You got your father's hair, that's for sure."

"Is that a bad thing?"

Marjorie chuckles at his question. "No, it's not bad. It's *beautiful.*"

When I look at Nikita, she's wiping tears from her eyes. Like me, she's moved by their reunion. She's refreshingly different from Azrael, who manages to look emotionless through the entire thing.

Marjorie urgently requests, "Tell me something about yourself. Tell me *anything!*"

"Well, I visit you all the time," Alexander says. "Do you remember Pebbles, the black cat that followed you home all those years ago?"

Swatting his arm, his mom cries, "*Of course* I remember Pebbles!"

"I was the one who encouraged Pebbles to follow you home. I thought you needed a friend," Alexander says. "Also, Pebbles lives with me now, so you'll be able to see him soon."

Fresh tears surge down her face at the thought of reuniting with Pebbles. Marjorie throws her arms around her son and cries into his sweater.

"Don't cry, Mom!" Alexander exclaims. "You should be happy."

"I *am* happy. These are happy tears!"

"Oh."

When Alexander wraps her in his arms, I smile from ear-to-ear. So far, this might be the best part of my job. I don't want to interrupt their reunion, so I sidle closer to Azrael and whisper, "Nikita and I were both crying. How do you manage to look so stony all the time?"

"Because I've done this for a very long time, Miss Alvarez."

Miss Alvarez. I wish he'd call me Lucy. Even Larry started calling me Lucy after awhile. *Miss Alvarez* sounds too formal. Haven't we been working together long enough for him to be a bit less—

Azrael's voice interrupts my thoughts. "Stony as I am, that doesn't mean I'm not touched by their reunion... *Lucy.*"

Azrael gives me a little grin that would probably melt the hearts of his many fans.

Chapter Twelve

THE NEXT TIME I SEE Azrael, he's in a black leather jacket with his hair slicked back. I know he can hear my thoughts sometimes, so I shouldn't be thinking he looks hot, but he *does*. And he looks more dangerous than usual.

I start a conversation before my thoughts get too weird. "So, uh... do you think I'll ever get to work with Nikita? She seemed really sweet."

"Perhaps." Azrael's voice is rife with boredom, as always. "When you complete your training with me, you're welcome to get in contact with her. However... Helpers usually work alone. I should have told you that sooner."

Alone? That sounds so boring. I would prefer to have a partner. "When will my training be over?" I ask.

"Your training will be over when I decide you're capable of doing this on your own... and frankly, you're far from it."

My bottom lip dips into a pout when I hear his answer. Does he think I'm a slow learner? Should I be further along than I am?

"If you recall... on our last mission, I didn't stop Oliver from taking his own life because he was terminally ill and suffering," Azrael says. "Today, we *will* be stopping a suicide... or we'll attempt to, at least. Are you ready, Lucy?"

When he calls me *Lucy* again, my pout is overturned by a smile. However, my smile is short-lived. Azrael takes us to a young guy's bedroom, and he has a gun on his lap.

"Oh my god!" I gasp. When he raises it to his head, I try to knock it out of his hand, but my fist passes through him. "Oh my god, *don't*! Don't do it!"

"Please remain calm," Azrael advises me. "Jason has been contemplating suicide for several days. We came here today because he seems more determined than ever to go through with it. This is the first time he's actually taken his father's gun from his bedroom."

Calm? Azrael wants me to remain calm? How is he not panicking? The gun is still pressed against Jason's forehead, so I scream at him, "*Doooon't!*" When he lowers the gun back to his lap, relief surges through me. I thought we were going to fail the mission before it had even started.

"The young man's name is Jason Dorsey," Azrael says. "You can read about him on your LightTab, if you wish, but I've had my eye on him for a few days now, so I might as well fill you in. About a week ago, his situation took a turn for the worse. First, he wasn't accepted into Brown University, where his then-girlfriend will be attending college next year."

Raising an eyebrow, I ask, "His *then*-girlfriend?"

"That's right. His girlfriend, Sophia, broke up with him a few days after he got his rejection letter. They had been together for two years."

"What a bitch!" The words fly out of me, and I don't regret it.

Azrael says, "Their break-up had nothing to do with colleges. She told Jason she had feelings for one of his friends."

"What... a... *bitch*," I reiterate. I'm totally on Jason's side. He has a lot going for him. To begin with, he's really cute. He's got two of the palest blue eyes I've ever seen, and it's an interesting contrast with his dark skin. He's got the physique that most guys wish they had. If he killed himself over an ex-girlfriend, that would be such a waste.

"Jason lives with his mother, father, a sister who adores him, and a little brother who idolizes him," Azrael reports. "If he left them, I believe they would be crushed. We need to distract him long enough that he changes his mind."

I bring my lips to Jason's ear and yell, *"Do... not... kill yourself!"*

I have an uncle who committed suicide, and it broke my dad's heart forever. Poor Dad. He's lost so many people. I should probably check on him soon.

Jason's trying to hold back tears, but I can see them shuddering in his eyes. He keeps stroking the gun, almost lovingly, as if to convince himself it's the solution he needs.

I try to give him a pep talk. "You'll meet other girls. You'll love other people! As for school... who cares? Maybe that wasn't the right college for you. Maybe you'll have an even better experience at the school you *do* go to? Maybe that's where you'll meet the love of your life and you'll be glad it all worked out the way it did? I know it hurts right now, but it will get better eventually! You have *so* much more to live for than that stupid Sophia."

I catch a glimpse of a slight smile on Azrael's lips. I hope that means he approved of my motivational speech? Unfortunately, it had no effect on Jason, who presses the gun against his head again.

In a panic, I ask my instructor, "Oh no, what do we do?"

"Like I said, we need a distraction. I have an idea." Azrael charges from the room and returns a moment later, led by the Dorsey family's ginger cat. The cat leaps onto Jason's lap, and he lowers his gun again.

Jason scratches the cat's head and whispers, "What are you doing, Nacho? Are you trying to talk me out of this?"

Nacho responds with a purr, blissfully unaware of his human's foul mood.

"I'm going to suggest something else, but I don't think you're going to like it," Azrael says.

I give him an eye roll before he reveals his plan. "Uh oh. What is it?"

"The ex, Sophia... Jason's been texting her all day, but she hasn't replied to him." Azrael points at the phone next to Jason's knee. "We can go to the girlfriend and encourage her to reply."

"Why would we do that?" I screech. "We wouldn't want to get them back together!"

"No, that's not our goal... but if he hears from her again, it might ease some of his pain." Azrael waits for me to reply, but all I do is blink at him. Nacho was a much better plan than Sophia. I don't know Jason's ex, but I already don't like her.

Azrael asks, "What do you think? Should we try it?"

"I mean, I *guess*," I surrender. "It seems like a temporary solution, though... and what if it makes things worse?"

"Another spirit will likely have a hand in Jason's love life at a later date. Right now, our *only* job is to get him to put the gun away. Sophia might be our best bet."

Azrael is supposed to be the master at this. If he has an idea, who am I to question him? As soon as I give him a nod, he takes us to Sophia's room. Jason's ex is a real basic-looking chick with way too much makeup and a fake ass tan. She doesn't look like she'd be worth Jason's heartache.

"She's already on her phone, so... see if you can get her to send a text to Jason," Azrael encourages me.

"*Me*? But this was *your* idea!"

"Please don't be petulant, Miss Alvarez. Remember, I'm still your instructor."

Oh crap. Has he downgraded me to *Miss Alvarez* again? I must be getting on his nerves.

"*Jason!*" I shout at Sophia. "Text Jason! Aren't you curious to know how he is? Jason, Jason, Jason, Jason, Jason!"

My nagging gets instant results. She immediately sends a text to her suffering ex-boyfriend.

Sry I haven't been replying. I have a lot on my mind and I'm just trying to figure things out. We can still talk if you want.

We warp back to Jason to see how he's handling the text. Nacho—my hero—is still on his lap. This cat is such a good guardian, he's putting us to shame.

Jason reads Sophia's text, but doesn't respond. In fact, he tosses his phone, banishing it to the end of his bed.

I point out to Azrael, "Uh... I don't think your plan helped."

"Perhaps. The cat seems to be working, though," Azrael says. "Also, Jason's thoughts are a little less morbid now. Earlier, he was thinking about his blood splattered on the wall."

"Yikes."

"Now he's thinking about dinner. That's a good sign. Do you have any other ideas?"

Jason's fingers aren't far from his gun, so we're definitely not in the clear. Sighing, I ask Azrael, "You said he has a brother and sister, right?"

"Right. He has two younger siblings. Jasmin is eight and Isaak is twelve."

"Maybe we could send one of them to check on Jason?" I suggest. "Seeing his sister's face might change his mind."

"Good idea," he commends me. "One of us should keep an eye on Jason, and one of us should fetch the girl. Which job do you want?"

I volunteer to stay with Jason, and as soon as Azrael is out of the room, I swat our charge's arm. I'm sure it doesn't feel it, but it gives me satisfaction anyway.

"*What* are you thinking?" I lecture him. "Why would you think about killing yourself because things got a little bad? Do you know how much I would have loved to trade places with you? Do you know how much I would have loved to be healthy? I never even got to *think* about going to college! You're lucky to have a mom and a dad, but you don't even know it! Why would you even think about breaking their hearts over this?"

When a little girl with braids suddenly pops her head into the room, Jason hides his gun behind him.

"Mom says it'll be time for dinner in ten minutes," Jasmin says. "Also, Isaak needs your help with his homework."

Jason acknowledges the request with a slow nod. "Okay."

"We're having fish." Jasmin snorts.. "I *hate* fish. Yuck."

Her brother says, "It's not so bad. At least it's not shrimp."

"Shrimp. Yuck!" Jasmin shudders at the thought. "I wish Dad didn't like seafood because that's why we have it all the time. Mom makes it a lot because he likes it a lot."

"Or maybe Mom just likes to torture you?" suggests a winking Jason. "Look... you can tell Isaak I'll help him after dinner."

Jasmin bobs her head and races from the room. When he's alone again, Jason picks up the gun and heaves a sigh.

"I guess death'll have to wait for another day," Jason whispers to himself—then he returns the stolen gun to his dad's room.

Success. When I try to give Azrael a high five, he looks at me like I've lost my mind.

"The little sister was a good idea," Azrael says.

"I know." I manifest a box of Reese's Pieces and sprinkle a few into my mouth. "Your cat idea wasn't bad, though. Can you imagine if he actually *had* killed himself? His little brother and sister would have been traumatized for life."

"I know. That's why we had to prevent it. We should probably check on him in a day or two, to make sure Jason hasn't changed his mind." When he reaches for my wrist, I assume we're going to warp. "Until then... we have more missions to do."

Chapter Thirteen

I HAVE ZERO TIME TO rest between missions. According to Azrael, it's not uncommon for a Helper to take on two, three, or even a dozen jobs in a single day. It makes sense, I guess. People are dying all the time, and if you're a Helper, your work is never done.

I wonder if I should take my mom's concerns into consideration. Normal guidework is usually a lot less depressing, and there's no pressure to take on multiple jobs. This might be more than I can handle.

When Azrael takes me to a rest home, I have to hold back a sigh. This is going to be sad, isn't it? I just *know* it's going to be sad.

The first person we see is an old woman in a wheelchair. Her tiny shoulders are swallowed up by an oversized pink sweater, and she has a baby doll on her lap.

The woman waves to me with a palsied hand and says, "Hello, dear!"

At first, I think she's talking to someone behind me, but there's no one in the hall but her, me and Azrael.

"This is the dementia wing," Azrael explains. "Dementia patients have hallucinations, but they can also see us... sometimes. The same goes for humans hovering close to death. The closer they are, the easier it is for them to catch a glimpse."

"Hi!" I wave to the old lady and give her my most beaming smile. "Is that your baby doll?"

"This is June," the lady says. "I gave birth to her exactly twenty-one years ago today."

"Wow," I reply, because I don't know what else to say. Azrael's sidling past her wheelchair, so I guess she isn't our charge. As I follow him, I give the lady a pat on her shoulder and add, "Well, she's lucky to have a mom like you."

Azrael and I hurry down the hall and turn into another room, where there's a big guy hunched over in his wheelchair. His tan face is mostly unlined, and a lot of his hair is still black, untouched by age. When I check my LightTab, I'm surprised to find out he's actually in his seventies.

"If you haven't figured it out already, this man is our charge," Azrael says. "His name is Paul Cisternino, he's seventy-four, and he's in the advanced stages of dementia. He can't walk, can't sit up on his own, and he can barely feed himself. Something inside of him is still afraid of death, so we're here to help him with his fear."

Azrael kneels in front of Paul and gently takes his hand. Our charge must be able to see him, because he looks a bit spooked.

"It's alright, Mr. Cisternino. You'll be leaving this body soon, but you don't need to be afraid," Azrael says. "Your guardian angels and spirit guides are with you, and I promise you, you *will* be reunited with your wife. Cathy's missed you. Your mom and dad have missed you. Release your fear so they can come to you."

He doesn't seem like the usual Azrael. I'm in awe. The first time I felt this way, he was talking to Simone after she lost her baby. There's something so comforting about him when he gets like this. He seems *truly* angelic.

When Azrael stands and starts poking on his LightTab, I'm standing behind him, so I can see the screen. He starts playing an old song called *In the Still of the Night,* and within the first few seconds, Paul starts to cry.

"He can hear that?" I ask.

"Yes. And it's his favorite song. He and his wife danced to this song on their wedding day. I thought it might give him some comfort."

Paul's head starts swaying back and forth. Something about the music seems to have touched something inside of him.

In the middle of the song, a young caregiver sweeps into the room and says, in a gratingly singsong voice, "Aww, what's giving you the weepies, Paul?" Steering his wheelchair from the room, she adds, "Come on. I'm taking you to lunch. It's potato salad day. Does that sound good or *what?*"

Paul doesn't respond, and his eyes stay on Azrael as long as they can.

"I'm sensing some stubbornness in him. It may yet be awhile until he passes," Azrael says. "I'll keep checking on him, and when he's closer to death, we'll return."

"That sounds so morbid."

"Sorry," he apologizes. "I tend to be blunt."

I'm curious about mealtime, so I follow Paul's wheelchair to a small common room, filled with tables and chairs. The lady steers his chair to one of the tables, and within a minute or two, his meal arrives. It doesn't look as bad as I expected. There's a club sandwich, condiments, a fruit cup, and a plate of colorful potato salad. Paul grabs his fork, but he doesn't do anything with it. I wonder if he's forgotten how to use it. Frustrated, he returns it to his plate and tackles the sandwich instead.

Looking about the room, I start to feel super depressed. Most of the home's residents are octogenarians, or even older. I've always felt a bit bitter about dying young, but now that I'm here, I don't think it's much better to die old.

A nurse tries to coach him on how to use his fork. He mumbles a reply, snorts at her, and starts to feed himself without any assistance.

When Azrael finally swaggers into the room, I go over to him and ask, "Is there *anything* we can do to help him?"

"I can help him remember, but the effects would only be temporary," Azrael says. "When he's closer to death, and his children are with him, I'll help him."

"You can bring back his memories?" When Azrael gives me a nod, I ask, "*How?*"

"It's a very advanced technique. Only a handful of angels and Archangels are capable of it," Azrael says. "Because of its temporary effects, it doesn't qualify as a miracle, but... it's close."

"You impress me," I tell him. He looks surprised by that, and so am I. It sounded unintentionally flirty, but now that it's out of my mouth, I might as well expand on my thoughts. "I'm serious. There's so much you can do, and even though you try to act like none of this bothers you, I can tell that you *really* care about people. It's hard to not be in awe of you."

"I appreciate that, but..." Azrael's jaw starts twitching. It's kind of cute that my compliments had that effect on him. "I'm sure you would feel that way about any of the Archangels."

"I don't think so," I object. "I met Jophiel, and he didn't seem that impressive."

"That's probably because you've heard about his reputation... which, by the way, he's trying to clean up. Trust me, Lucy, as far as Archangels go, I'm hardly extraordinary."

"Well, I guess I'll have to start hanging out with more Archangels. When are you going to introduce me to your friends?"

Oh wow. Now it *really* sounds like I'm flirting with him—and here, of all places.

"That depends." A fleeting smirk turns his lips as he echoes, "When are you going to introduce me to *your* friends?"

"You mean... my friends that *don't exist*?"

"You have friends. I know you had some when you were alive," Azrael says. "Not to mention, I saw you with Samuel the other day."

"You know Sam?"

"Of course. He works in an Asylum *and* he's an angel. Why wouldn't I know him?"

For some reason, talking about Sam makes me go quiet. When I turn my attention back to Paul, he's sitting with a woman who looks way too young to be here.

"That's one of his daughters," Azrael replies, as if he's reading my mind—and he probably is.

The daughter quizzes him, "Dad, do you know my name?"

He stares at her, wide-eyed and blinking, with his fork still in his hand.

"Come on. Think about it," she challenges him. "You remember me, don't you?"

Paul mumbles a barely audible reply. "Helen?"

The woman shakes her head and expels a sigh. I have a feeling she's been through this before. "No, Dad, Helen is your sister. I'm Carmen, remember?"

There's no spark of recognition in his eyes. Copying her sigh, he goes back to eating his potato salad.

I ask Azrael, "Can't you help him *now*?"

"I promise you, I *will* help him... at the right time. For now, all we should do is watch." After a short pause, he adds, "You're a sweet girl, Lucy. I think it's nice that you always want to help people. You have a good, kind soul."

His praise pushes my lips into a giddy smile. I wasn't expecting *him* to compliment *me*.

After lunch, Carmen takes her dad to the in-home salon for a haircut. To be honest, he kind of needs one.

I wonder if it's the last haircut he'll ever get?

"We should go," Azrael says. "Like I said, when he's closer to death, we'll return. For now, we should focus our attention on other missions."

"Okay."

I'm still beaming at Azrael's compliments. I know I smile a lot, but this is different.

It feels like I might smile forever.

Chapter Fourteen

AZRAEL AND I HOP FROM one mission to another to another. I think he's trying to demonstrate the work load that's expected of a Helper, but frankly, I'm exhausted. I'm not physically exhausted—in fact, I don't think it's possible to get physically exhausted anymore. Mentally, however, I'm totally drained.

On our next mission, we visit a pair of expectant parents. Sadly, their baby died while they were sleeping, and Azrael and I are here to collect the soul and take it Home. Azrael shows me how to make the light bubble around the baby's tiny body. I didn't think I'd be able to do it, but with concentration, it was easier than I thought.

"You're a quick learner, Lucy." This time, Azrael's praise is followed by unfair criticism. "I do have concerns about your state of mind, however. You've been depressed on many of these missions."

"I've been depressed because this is depressing!" I argue. I know he wants me to become numb like him, but I don't think I could ever stop feeling sympathy for a mother or father who's lost their child. If it ever stopped depressing me, I would no longer be Luciana Alvarez. I would be some unrecognizable shell of myself.

When he says we'll be taking the baby to Asylum Seventeen, Sam immediately springs into my mind. I wonder if we'll run into him?

Azrael encourages me to practice warping, since I'm familiar with our destination. Warping is a required skill since I'll be expected to go on many missions by myself. For some reason, my first attempt sends us to a McDonald's on East 17th Avenue in Columbus, Ohio. I laugh it off and try again.

"You need to practice more," Azrael lectures me, even though my second attempt is successful. "When I'm not with you, you should *always* be practicing basic skills like manifestation and warping."

"First of all, my first instructor told me that warping *wasn't* a basic skill."

"It's basic for a Helper."

I ignore his comeback and continue, "Secondly... how am I supposed to practice those skills when you're *always* with me? I have no time to myself whatsoever."

He gives me a vacant, cold stare and asks, "Are you complaining about my company?"

"No. I like your company. It's just... it would be nice to have a break from time to time."

We deliver the new baby to an angel named Jessica, who asks, "Does the child have a name?" I have no idea, so I look to Azrael for an answer.

"His parents were going to call him Finn."

"Good. It's always a bit awkward when the parents haven't decided on a name yet," Jessica says.

"What happens when there isn't a name?" I ask.

She replies, "The angels usually get together and decide on an appropriate one. In most cases, it isn't necessary."

Jessica seems nice, but I'm a little disappointed that Sam's not working in the nursery today. Maybe I'll run into him before Azrael and I set off on yet another mission?

"If you want a break, I'll give you a break," Azrael says. "But I need to speak to you tomorrow."

My brow pinches as I follow him out of the nursery. "That sounds ominous. Are you going to tell me something bad?"

"Maybe. Maybe not. That's why I'm telling you tomorrow instead of now."

Azrael's strides are long, so I have to double my pace to keep up with him. "Hey... do Helpers ever go on normal missions? I've always wondered that. Is it always about death, or can we sometimes take a break and help a teenage boy find his first girlfriend?" That's what I did on my very first mission, and it remains one of my favorites.

"Sometimes... allowances can be made," Azrael says.

"That's good to know, because I—" My reply is cut short when we walk into the next room and I see Sam locking lips with a guy. "Wait, is that..."

"Sam's boyfriend," Azrael fills in the blanks for me. "I thought you might be fond of Sam. Perhaps I should have told you sooner?"

Oh wow. Suddenly, I feel like such an idiot. I had convinced myself of Sam's interest in *me*, but maybe there was a reason he never used the word "date?" I was crushing on him a little bit, but I'm not as disappointed as I could be. Sam and his boyfriend look like a nice couple, and lately, I find myself drawn to Azrael.

Is that crazy? It's not like I could *ever* be with the Angel of Death.

I say goodbye to Azrael, draw a fortifying breath, and march over to introduce myself to Sam's hot boyfriend.

"Hi." I stick out a hand and hope I don't look too awkward. "I'm Lucy, a friend of Sam. I'm not interrupting anything important, am I?"

"Not at all. I'm Kaleb." He shakes my hand and flashes a dimpled smile. Kaleb is really handsome. Black-haired, blue-eyed and bearded, he looks a little older than Sam—not that age seems to be a big issue here. "Sam is my—"

I try to guess the rest of his sentence. "Boyfriend. I know. Azrael told me."

Sam looks totally oblivious to the fact that I've just been punched in the gut by this news. I don't think he was trying to play me, I just think I was horribly naive.

"How long have you been together?" I ask.

When Sam replies, "Fifty years," I almost scream. They both look so young, it's easy to forget they're actually a *lot* older than me.

"That's a serious commitment!" I exclaim. "I haven't had a boyfriend for one day, let alone, fifty years."

"You'll have a boyfriend if you want one," Sam assures me. "You're such a pretty girl, after all. Don't you think she's stunning, Kaleb?"

When Kaleb concurs, I feel even dumber. My gay friend in middle school was the *only* guy who always told me I was pretty. Why did I just assume Sam was hitting on me when he said the same thing?

We chat a little while about the nursery, baby Finn, and my strange obsession with Reese's Pieces. Kaleb says he prefers M&Ms, so I give him a disapproving glare. After all the time I've spent with Azrael, I feel like I've been honing my glare.

I say goodbye to the boys, and as I leave Asylum Seventeen, I burst into a fit of giggles.

Sam's gay. Azrael's off-limits.

I'm really awesome at choosing my crushes, aren't I?

Chapter Fifteen

AS I LISTEN TO MY MOM complain about failing her latest mission, my mind drifts to Azrael. A girl like me having a crush on an Archangel is like a fangirl crushing on a celebrity. I can fantasize all I want, but it's never going to happen.

I can't believe I wasn't attracted to him from day one—in fact, it took me awhile to understand why Azrael was so idolized by his fans. Honestly, what's not to like? He's tall, broody and mysterious. If you dig a little deeper, he's gentle and caring too. Now that Sam is off the menu, I think my crush on Azrael has officially fired up.

I need to be mindful of my thoughts when I'm around him, though. I wouldn't want him peeking into my head and realizing I feel this way. Besides, he's still my instructor. Maybe it's not as weird as the time I had a crush on my 8th grade chemistry teacher, but it still feels a little inappropriate to imagine what he looks like under his clothes.

Actually, I *can* see what he looks like under his clothes. A quick search on the LightTab pulls up several shirtless pictures him—and yeah, I've saved a few. At first, I remember thinking he was too thin, but now his lean muscles are growing on me.

I don't know why you can find shirtless pics of so many Archangels. I think they enjoy having fangirls and fanboys.

When a squawk from my mom interrupts my thoughts, I realize I missed at least half of her story. "Can you believe that? He deliberately sabotaged the mission because he didn't like where it was heading!"

I have no idea what she's talking about. I feel bad that I haven't been paying attention, but I catch enough keywords to give her a reply. "Yeah, that wasn't cool at all."

"No. It wasn't." My mom stomps around the room in a rage. "You know I don't like to fail. This is the first one I've failed in a *long* time, Luciana!"

"That really sucks." While I'm pretending to relate to my mom's rage, I get a text from the guy who's enslaved my thoughts.

Practice your warping and come to Archangel Tower. The guard should let you enter.

"Well, Mom, I guess I have to go." I hold up my text from Azrael, even though she's too far away to read it. "Duty calls."

"Alright." She collapses on the couch and dismisses me with a hand flick. "Hopefully you won't be busy all day again. It would be nice to have dinner with you... for once."

I know she wants me to quit my Helper training, and sometimes I agree with her, but it gives me something to be proud of. Not a lot of people can say they've gotten hands-on training from an Archangel.

After a successful warp, I'm greeted by a friendly female guard who permits me through the gate with a nod. I find my way to Azrael's office without too much trouble. Before I can knock, I hear him shout, "Come in, Lucy."

I enter and close the door behind me. Azrael's wearing a white t-shirt and distressed jeans, and his hair's more disheveled than usual. It's the most basic outfit in the world, and he probably didn't brush his hair today, but he still manages to look sexy.

Stop thinking this. Archangels can hear your thoughts, I remind myself.

"Hello, Miss Alvarez. You can sit, if you'd like, but this shouldn't take too long."

I feel a little flop in my belly when he says that. His tone's even hollower than usual, and it doesn't bode well for me.

"What's up?" I ask, trying to sound positive.

"Miss Alvarez, I'm releasing you from your duties as a Helper."

Oh no. I *knew* it would be something like this! I've had a bad feeling since yesterday. Keeping my cool, I ask, "So... I failed my training?"

"No, you didn't fail. I just don't know if you have what it takes for this job."

Azrael's face is inexpressive, as usual. He doesn't care that he's just broken my heart with this. It'll be my mom's dream come true, but it's not what I wanted.

"Why did you decide this? Can I get some kind of explanation?"

Azrael starts his evaluation with a sigh. "Your empathy is good, but to be a Helper, you need a certain degree of detachment. You need to be more level-headed under pressure, but you were depressed or upset on most of our missions. When you asked for a break, I was afraid the work load was getting to you. I think you'd be happier taking on regular missions."

"Why?" My voice has gone a bit whiny, so I try to dial it back a bit. "Why do you get to decide that for me?"

His tongue makes a snide tutting noise. "Because I'm Archangel Azrael. That's why."

"I know. But if you had any respect for me at all, you would have talked this over with me before dropping a bomb like this! Why won't you give me a chance to tell you how much I want this... or that I'll work *really* hard to prove myself? I know it probably seems like I care too much, but... maybe I could learn how to detach myself a little more? Maybe—"

"Miss Alvarez..." Azrael interrupts me as he rises from his chair. "I'm sorry, but I've already made my decision, and no argument from you is likely to change my mind. I truly believe this will make you happier in the long run."

"No. It won't." I'm shook. I can't believe this is happening. My mind is racing, desperate to find a way to change his mind. I don't want this to be the last time I see him. "What about our mission with Paul? We never got to finish it!"

"I'll finish it on my own. Now... I really need to go."

"*Please!*" I beg. I feel silly for sounding so desperate, but I have to try. "Just give me one more chance. *One*. Will you think about it? I know what I have to do now. I know I—"

Azrael warps from his office before I can say another word to save myself.

Chapter Sixteen: Azrael

I HAD TO LET HER GO. I couldn't stand the effect she had on me. It was intoxicating to be near her, beautiful distraction that she was. Her bright smiles, her compassion, her sweetness—she was everything a man could want. It's been a week since I said goodbye to Lucy Alvarez, and I still think of her constantly.

I couldn't let myself fall for her. Had I let it flourish, it would have been an all-consuming love, the kind that occupies my mind at every hour of the day. I couldn't risk it. My job is too important. It requires all of my focus. Even now, a week later, I'm still distracted. It doesn't help that Lucy sends daily texts to remind me of her.

I know I'm not your Helper anymore, but could we still watch a movie together sometime?

Have I convinced you to reconsider yet?

I know you're ignoring me... but I miss spending time with you.

She only sends one each day, but it's enough to keep me thinking of her. I can't give in, no matter how much I miss the sight of her face, nor can I bring myself to delete her from my contacts. Deep down, I know I like getting these little messages from her. I wonder how long she'll keep sending them if she never gets a response?

I miss her as well. There's a part of me that thinks I'm an idiot for pushing her away, because girls like Lucy are a rarity. I haven't loved anyone for a very long time, nor have I wanted to fall in love. I know what love does to me. It transforms me. I cannot afford to turn into a lovesick puppy who only thinks of Lucy. Before I let her go, I was already thinking of her far too much.

Worse yet—I know she has feelings for me as well. I keep imagining what might have happened if I hadn't pushed her away.

When Michael invites me on a stroll around Archangel Tower, a rare chuckle slips out of me. Every now and then, he likes to step outside and meander around the gate, in full view of his screaming fangirls. Michael seems like the most confident man in the world, but people would be surprised by how insecure he is. He thrives on fangirl cheers and squeals.

I meet Michael at the entrance, and as soon as we step outside, there's a crescendo of adoring howls. They're most excited to see Michael, I'm sure, but I suspect I might have a few fans as well.

"So... Azrael..." Michael addresses me with tension in his voice. "I wanted to speak to you about some... concerns."

"Concerns about what?"

Before I get an answer, a few girls scream in ear-piercing unison, *"We love you, Michael!"* A moment later, their volume is challenged by a second group yelling, *"We love you, Azrael!"* It's flattering, to say the least, but I doubt I've done anything to deserve their devotion.

It's a good thing we're separated by a gate. If that barrier didn't exist, Michael would get swarmed and tackled.

"I have some concerns about Jophiel," Michael says. "After his trial, he won't speak to me. He won't even look at me! My attempt to dole out justice may cause irreparable damage to our relationship."

I give him an honest answer, as I always do. "The trial was a bit over-the-top. The matter could have been settled quietly. Instead, you turned it into a spectacle, and his name was raked through the mud."

"So says the man who arrested him," Michael says. "How are *you* on good terms with Jophiel when I'm not?"

"Jophiel and I have always been close, and it wasn't my idea to arrest him. I was carrying out *your* order."

"Well... how can I get back in his good graces?"

I give him a piece of painfully obvious advice. "Apologize?"

Michael rejects the idea with a snort. "If I apologized, I would have to admit I was wrong, and I wasn't wrong. His behavior was highly suspect!"

A smile breezes across Michael's lips when he glances at his fans. He can pretend to be immune to their adulation, but I know he enjoys the attention.

All of a sudden, he changes the subject. "Should we go sign a few autographs? What do you think?"

I almost tell him I'm too busy, but I suppose it couldn't hurt. It's been a long time since I've spared any time for the crowd at the gate. When we approach, our fans queue up and stick photos of us through the bars. I manifest a pen and start signing my name in silver ink.

While I'm signing a picture for a heavily freckled young man, he asks me, "Does Archangel Haniel ever come out here?"

Truthfully, we rarely step outside. We usually warp to and from the tower, but I don't want to dash his hopes. "Occasionally, yes."

"Is she still dating Chris Pho?" When I give him a nod, the boy says, "I hope he knows how lucky he is!"

I move down the line, signing autograph after autograph. I try to be friendly, though I feel a bit flustered. Crowds have always made me nervous, and I never know how to react to compliments. One young lady tells me I "have the greatest cheekbones ever." How am I supposed to respond to that? If I thank her, it might sound as if I agree. If I reject her compliment, I might look like an arse.

Unlike me, Michael seems to be enjoying himself. He's a lot more comfortable speaking to strangers than I am. By comparison, I'm a bashful, awkward mess.

After a few minutes of signing autographs, I suddenly spot Lucy on the other side of the gate. When our eyes meet, I try to look as indifferent as I can.

As I'm signing another young lady's picture, I ask Miss Alvarez, "What are you doing here?" If I could speak quietly, I would, but the chatter of fans makes whispering impossible.

"You won't answer my texts, so I thought I'd come here and see if the guard at the gate would let me in."

"It appears he didn't."

"No." Lucy exaggerates a pout. "No, he definitely didn't."

Lucy looks as lovely as ever. Her brown hair's pulled back in a ponytail, and her pink dress is fit for a doll. She's so pretty, I'm tempted to change my mind and beg her to join me on my next mission.

But I can't. I *won't.*

"I really wish you would have given me another chance, Azrael. Was I really *that* bad?" she asks.

Our conversation seems to interest a few young ladies standing nearby. I hope they don't think we're discussing anything scandalous.

"No. You did well," I reply. "I made my decision based on what I thought was best for you."

"But it's *not!*" Lucy cries. "I really enjoyed working with you. Yeah, the missions were depressing sometimes, but the work was fulfilling. When I was with you, I... for the first time ever, I felt like someone important. I felt like I mattered!"

I shake my head and sign another autograph. I'm not sure what she expects me to say.

"I won't bother you again. This will be the last time," Lucy says. "I know I'm bugging you, I just... I'm really sad about what happened."

She's not bothering me at all. Seeing her face again has been a secret delight. "I'm sorry, Miss Alvarez. I didn't mean to make you upset."

I sign a few more autographs and dash away from the gate as quickly as I can. Lucy has no idea how unsettled I am, does she? She has no idea I think she's beautiful, charming, and a joy to be around.

I'm truly an idiot.

And I sincerely hope this isn't the last time I see her.

Chapter Seventeen: Luciana

AZRAEL MIGHT BE AN ass, but on the bright side, Sam and I have grown a lot closer. I even went out to dinner with Kaleb and him last night, and even though I felt like the third wheel, it's nice to have a couple of new friends.

After a bit of arm twisting, I convinced Sam to join me on a mission. He rarely takes a break from his Asylum duties, so I'm surprised I talked him into it. As soon as we arrive at our charge's house, I start venting to Sam. I've been holding a lot inside of me, and it all comes spilling out when Sam and I are alone together.

"It's bad enough that Azrael basically expelled me from his Helper school... but why is he ignoring me too? He doesn't respond to my texts, and he barely looked at me when I saw him in front of Archangel Tower the other day. Call me crazy, but I really thought we were getting along. I thought we were becoming friends. Was I stupid to think that? Be honest."

Sam responds kindly, even though he's probably tired of my raving. "I don't think you're stupid at all. I thought he liked you too, especially when he randomly showed up at *Flores* that one day. That couldn't have been a coincidence."

"I know, right? That's *exactly* what I thought!"

Sam and I just warped to a random living room. I don't see any sign of our charge yet, unless it's the basset hound sleeping on the rust orange armchair—which happens to be the oldest, ugliest piece of furniture I've ever seen in my life. A slit of sunshine peeking through the curtain is the only light in an otherwise dark room. This place is so musty and dim, it almost looks vacant.

Sam says, "To be honest, I was under the impression that Azrael had a thing for you."

"I don't know if I'd go *that* far, but I thought he enjoyed my company. I even got him to watch a movie with me... and he doesn't like movies." I heave a sigh that goes on way too long. "You know... I had a pretty major crush on him."

"I know," replies a winking Sam. "I could tell."

"Am I just totally stupid? I shouldn't have let myself have feelings for him at all," I admonish myself. "Now I'm just one of his many fangirls. How sad is that?"

Sam wraps an arm around my shoulders and gives me a one-armed hug. He's been really patient with me through all of this. I know he's probably tired of hearing about Azrael, but I can't help it. My need to rant is strong. "I've had my heart broken before," Sam admits. "This was a long time ago... before I met Kaleb. Back in the day, I was training to be an Archangel. Did I ever tell you that?"

I shake my head and answer, "Nope."

"Well, an Archangel named Jeremiel was overseeing my training. I had a *huge* crush on him. At one time, I even thought he was flirting with me, but it turned out I was *hugely* mistaken, and he was actually the reason I didn't become an Archangel. Even though my rating was high enough, he didn't recommend me for the position. He said my skills weren't good enough. I was heartbroken."

"That sounds like the same thing I went through."

"It's similar for sure. Anyway, do you want to know what I did after that? I took some time to myself... and then I met Kaleb. It turned out to be the best thing that ever happened to me. If I was an Archangel, I doubt I would have met him." Sam pokes me on the arm and says, "We just need to find you a Kaleb."

"Yeah. Maybe..."

I turn my attention to my LightTab and read about our charge. He's an eighty-year-old man named Joe Cotton. He's a retired mail carrier and a widower. His wife preceded him in death almost fifteen years ago, and he's been alone ever since. He has one son, but he lives in Australia, nine thousand miles away.

We need to locate Joe, but Sam's still talking about my failed love life. "It's hard to get over an Archangel," he says. "Believe me, I know. There's just something about them that draws you in and makes you obsess. They have a regal air. They ooze power. Once you've been close to one of them, everyone else seems to pale in comparison."

Bumping my shoulder against Sam's, I say, "*You* don't pale in comparison."

"And neither do you. Next time, we need to find you a guy who's actually worthy of you."

I hear a beeping noise in the adjacent room, so I follow the sound to a kitchen with mustard yellow walls. There, Joe Cotton is extracting a tv dinner from the microwave. Steam swirls from his meal as he pulls back the plastic that covers it.

Joe is a tall, black man with salt and pepper hair and a heavily lined face. He's wearing a Christmas sweater with snowflakes and reindeer on it, and he's got mismatched fuzzy slippers on his feet. His posture is stooped, he's got a bushy gray mustache, and a smile trembles on his lips as he stirs his mashed potatoes. There's something adorable about him. As soon as I see him, I feel motivated. I want good things to happen to him.

Like a pro, I take out my quartz crystal and attempt to listen to this thoughts. We need to know what our mission is, but right now, Joe's Salisbury steak is the only thing on his mind.

Joe's slippered feet scrape the floor as he dodders into the living room and collapses on a couch. His basset hound lifts his head, sniffs Joe's food, decides he doesn't care, and returns to his nap. The dog doesn't even look particularly concerned about Sam and me.

"So... what's our mission?" Sam asks.

"I don't know. I'm still trying to figure that out."

Joe turns on the tv and watches reruns of a black and white sitcom. I don't recognize it, but he must think it's funny, because he starts chuckling as soon as he turns it on.

On the table beside him, there's a portrait of a handsome, dark-skinned woman—I assume she's his wife. When he turns her picture to face the television, I suddenly feel like crying. Joe is a lonely old man, enjoying a packaged frozen dinner with a picture of his wife.

The crystal's still in my hand, so I catch a snippet of his thoughts.

I wish you were here with me, Rhonda. I always wish you were here.

"He's missing his wife," I report to Sam, even though I'm sure he can read minds a lot better than I can. "Should we bring her here to visit him? Is that our mission?"

"No. I'm sure Rhonda already visits him. It has to be something else," Sam says. "I think I know what our mission is, but I need to listen to his thoughts a little while longer to make sure I'm not missing anything."

I close my eyes and listen again.

I miss Tom, Rich, Harry... those were the good old days. My back hurts. The steak's still a little cold. I sure miss Rhonda's cooking.

I hear Joe's random thoughts, but none of them give me a clue about our mission. When he starts thinking about the characters on tv, I give up—for now, anyway.

I ask Sam, "What do you *think* our mission is?"

"I think he's lonely. I think it'll be our job to bring someone into his life."

Sam's probably right. I was thinking the same thing. We still need confirmation, so I clutch my crystal and listen.

Don't get out of the house much... need to get to the grocery store. Eggs and bread.

I shake my head and grumble. Our mission can't be something as lame as getting him to the grocery store and back, right? It needs to be something meaningful. It's *usually* meaningful.

"Maybe…" I reluctantly suggest something else. "Maybe we can get his son to visit him? Who are Tom, Rich and Harry? Do you have any idea?"

"They're his old friends," Sam says. "They all died before Joe. So far, his son hasn't crossed his mind."

"Do he and his son have a bad relationship?" I ask.

"I don't think so. I just think he lives really, *really* far away."

Joe finishes his meal, and when the sitcom ends, he leans back and closes his eyes.

I'm always by myself. Been alone a long time. Sometimes wish I had someone to talk to.

I swat Sam's arm when I hear that thought, because I'm sure he heard it too. We officially have our mission.

We need to find a companion for lonely Joe Cotton.

Chapter Eighteen: Azrael

A RIOT'S BROKEN OUT on the streets of New York City, and I'm one of four Archangels sent to quell it. Dark entities are drawn to rage and unrest. The riot will surely become a beacon for demons, and we must purge them before more chaos is seeded.

The Archangels are surprisingly cliquish. Michael rarely goes anywhere without Uriel, Raphael and Gabriel, while Raguel and Ariel are practically inseparable. My usual "crew," for lack of a better term, consists of Jophiel, Haniel, and Sandalphon. Jophiel and Haniel are more than capable of holding their own, in fact, the three of us are some of the highest ranking Archangels in terms of skill. However, I do worry about Sandalphon in situations like these. He's a decent fighter, but he has such an innocent face. I hate to see it seared by a shadowling's claws.

Cops in riot gear are staring down a horde of unruly civilians. So far, I don't see any sign of demonic activity, but that should change soon enough. As we wait for the enemy to appear, the others chat amongst themselves. I'm not much for small talk, so I'm rarely one to start a conversation.

Haniel's brought two of her most promising recruits to today's battle: Taishi Nakamura and Kaylene Bertonneau. Kaylene is Amber's daughter, and I believe she's only a few dozen missions away from attaining Archangel status. I don't know much about Taishi, but I know there was once some tension between Jophiel and him. Fortunately, they seem to be getting along.

Jophiel asks Taishi, "So, how are you and Leigh? Is your relationship still going strong? Is she still madly in love with you?"

Taishi, not unlike me, seems to be a quiet, private person. He answers with a sigh, "I don't know if I want to discuss that with you."

"Uh oh! Does that mean there's trouble in paradise?" Jophiel asks.

"No," Taishi says. "It means I don't want to discuss my relationship with Leigh's ex-boyfriend."

"Fair enough. I'll just assume everything is hunky-dory between you. If it wasn't, you'd be sulking more than usual." Thrusting a thumb at me, Jophiel adds, "If Leigh ever left you, you'd look even moodier than Azrael."

I respond to Jophiel's insult with a cold, hard stare.

"See? Doesn't he look sulky?" Turning to Haniel, Jophiel asks, "And how are you and Chris Pho? I miss him, you know."

"Everything's perfect." Haniel lowers her voice, but I can still hear every word she says. "But... the other day, he told me he loved me. Don't you think it's too soon for that?"

Jophiel says, "Not at all! I tell Anna I love her all the time, and we've been together as long as you and Chris."

My head shakes as I listen to their asinine chatter. It seems a bit silly to discuss one's love life in the middle of a riot. Jophiel tends to annoy me—probably because we're so different. Looking at Taishi's sour expression, I would guess he feels the same way.

"You guys are making me sad," Sandalphon whimpers.

Simultaneously, Jophiel and Haniel ask, "Why?"

"Because I don't have a girlfriend," Sandalphon whines. "Nobody likes Archangel Sandalphon. I don't even have proper fans like you do. I'm the least liked Archangel of all, I swear."

"Well, I can't really argue with that." Jophiel's remark earns him a punch on the arm from Haniel. "What? I'm just being honest with the boy."

"No. You're being *rude*," Haniel insists. "Sandalphon... why don't you ask out Kaylene? I think you'd be a good match."

Sandalphon studies Kaylene, and after a few seconds, he shakes his head. "No. I don't think she'd like me."

I make an obvious grunting noise. I hoped they would realize I'm tired of their chitchat, but the nonsense continues. In fact, it gets worse.

Jophiel asks, "What happened to your pretty Helper girl, Azrael? Have you made a move on her yet?"

"No. Nor do I intend to." I hope that answer satisfies him, because I've been trying to get Lucy off my mind.

"Well, you should. She was stunning, as I recall."

The conversation tapers off as the riot turns a lot more violent. Men in black hoodies uproot a road sign and hurl it at the cops. A flying bottle shatters on an officer's shield. Some arrests are made, and the cops start fighting back with their batons. Crowbars crash into a cop car's windshield, and sure enough, we see our first demons rising from the ground.

Jophiel rips his flaming sword from its sheath and says, too arrogantly for my taste, "I'll handle the first ones, if you don't mind." I guess his recent trial didn't teach him any humility.

As Jophiel banishes the first two demons, hundreds more start to rise and descend on the humans. A long-legged spider entity attaches itself to one of the cops. With a flick of my hand, I extract it, then drive my sword through its body.

We're quickly overrun, but it's nothing we can't handle. More than once, I've taken on entire hordes without any partner at my side. I charge into a throng of hissing shadows, swinging my sword as I run. These entities can't withstand even a single touch from my blade. The slightest brush turns their smoky bodies to dust.

I occasionally check on Sandalphon, because he always ends up with an injury or two. He seems to have teamed up with Taishi, oddly enough. Sandalphon paralyzes the demons, and Taishi runs them through. Jophiel and Kaylene seem to be working together too. They're standing back-to-back, making it impossible for any entities to approach from behind. For Archangel recruits, Kaylene and Taishi can unleash some impressive shock waves from their blades.

I whirl my sword, decimating several demons approaching my flank. Behind me, I hear a scream from Archangel Haniel. While she was attempting to extract a demon from one of the humans, a scorpion shadowling fired toxic black barbs into her back. I can smell her flesh burning as I race over to her and skewer the demon that attacked her.

"I'm alright," croaks a grimacing Haniel. "At least... I will be soon enough."

There's chaos in every direction, from both the rioters and the entities. It's been less than three minutes since the demons arrived, and I've already lost count of how many I've vanquished. When I glance at Sandalphon again, I'm surprised to discover it's actually Taishi who suffered an injury. His arm and shoulder have been blackened by a shadowling's bite. He's not quite an Archangel yet, so it will take him a bit longer to heal. I can only imagine how much pain he's in—but his face doesn't show it. I've got to admire him for that.

In the middle of the fight, I catch myself thinking about Lucy Alvarez. I wonder where she is, what she's doing, who she's with. This is the most inconvenient time to succumb to my even-more-inconvenient infatuation with her. I can't let her walk out of my life, can I? Am I really going to be that stupid?

I slay about a hundred demons on my own, and when the battle's over, Haniel's healed but Taishi hasn't. The rioters seem to have calmed down a bit as well, so we declare the mission a success.

As soon as we warp back Home, a squealing girl rushes over to Taishi and cries, *"Oh my god! Are you okay?"*

"I'm fine, Leigh-chan, it's... it's not as bad as it looks."

He's lying. Smoke is still seeping from his charred arm. It will probably take him an hour or two to heal a wound like that, and he'll be in excruciating pain the entire time.

The girl named Leigh asks, "Is this what every day will be like when you're an Archangel? Am I going to be worried about you *all the time?*"

"Not every day," Taishi corrects her. "Just... sometimes."

He should be honest with the girl. Daily encounters with demons are part of the job.

Jophiel claps a hand on my back and asks, "How many did you get? Did I outperform the Angel of Death today?"

Coolly, I reply, "If you had time to count them, you didn't outperform me."

"Cocky as ever," Jophiel says. "But... I suppose you've earned the right to be a bit cocky, eh? The same could be said about me. We're both incurably overconfident."

Jophiel says he needs to get back to Anna and dismisses himself. Sandalphon, whose nose got burnt during the fight, saunters away with slumping shoulders. I'm sure he won't be disfigured for too long, but it *does* look terrible. Only Jophiel, Kaylene and I made it through the battle without a scratch or burn. I'm not very familiar with the young lady, but she seems impressive.

Inevitably, Lucy is back on my mind. Like Sandalphon, I have no significant other to greet me after the fight.

I almost wish I did.

Chapter Nineteen: Luciana

HOW ARE WE SUPPOSED to complete this mission when Joe Cotton never leaves his house? It's day two, and he's only been outside once—to retrieve his newspaper from the porch. As we watch him shuffle through the house with the paper tucked under his arm, I tell Sam, "You know, I've never actually read a newspaper in my life. I used to get all of my news on social media. Is that bad?"

"No. In a way, you *still* get all of your news from social media." Sam holds up his LightTab and grins. "I don't know about you, but I *definitely* couldn't live without this little device."

Sam and I spent the last two hours trying to get Joe out of his house and into a space where he could encounter another human being. So far, nothing's worked. The house next door is vacant, so neighbors aren't an option. At noon, a guy comes to mow Joe's lawn, and for a moment, I wonder if he has friend potential. It was probably my best idea of the day, but Joe never stepped outside to greet him, and shouting at our charge doesn't seem to motivate him at all. I have a feeling this mission will be a long one.

"I'm sorry!" I've apologized to Sam at least three times today. I'm the one who begged him to go on a mission with me, and now he's stuck here. "Every hour you're here is an hour you're away from Asylum Seventeen. I'm so, *so* sorry!"

"You don't have to keep apologizing, Lu. It's okay," Sam says. He's the only one who's ever called me *Lu*, and it's kind of growing on me. "I probably needed a break from the Asylum. I love children, but when you're around them all the time, they can start to make you a bit mad."

"Mad as in crazy, right?"

Sam chuckles at my question. "Yes. Were you imagining me losing my patience and blowing up at the children? That wouldn't be very angelic of me, would it?"

When Joe starts clipping coupons, it gives me some hope. Maybe he's got plans to do some shopping in the near future? "Hey... didn't Joe say something about getting groceries?"

"He didn't say it, but he did *think* it. It seems you're quite good at reading minds."

"You think so? Larry did say it was one of the areas where I excelled."

Sam raises a blonde eyebrow. "Larry?"

"My old instructor. He was a gangster."

"Really?" Sam throws back his head and chuckles at that. "My dear, sweet Lucy learned her tricks from a gangster? That's almost impossible to imagine."

"We got along pretty well, actually. I think he cleaned up his act in the afterlife." I lean over Joe's shoulder to see what kind of coupon he's clipping. It's a *buy five save a dollar* coupon for tv dinners. The microwave seems to provide him with most of his meals.

I've got my hand in my pocket, and it's next to my quartz crystal, so I accidentally catch a glimpse of his thoughts.

Really liked those Salisbury steaks. Got to get me more of those.

I feel kind of sad that he's getting excited about a meal in a box, but I use this to my advantage. "*Yes!*" I exclaim. "Yes, *please* go pick up some more of those, Joe! Go, go, go!"

This time, my attempt at cheerleading gets him out of his chair and moving to the door, where he collects his coat and keys. Unlike Azrael, Sam indulges me when I try to give him a high five.

As we follow Joe to his car, I tell Sam, "You know, you're a lot more pleasant to work with than Azrael."

"I can imagine," Sam agrees. "He's a bit prickly, isn't he? He always seems that way when I interact with him."

"I hate to say anything nice about him after he fired me, but... he's not so bad. He seems like he would be cold, but there's something gentle about him too." I shrug at my assessment. "He always said the most comforting things to people who lost their children... or to people who were sick. There were a lot of layers to his personality. He—"

Sam interrupts me. "Your crush on him is even bigger than you're letting on, isn't it?"

"No!" I deal a light slap to Sam's arm for suggesting such a thing. "Okay... maybe. It *was* big. I don't know if it's so big anymore."

"You probably got even more enamored with him after he pushed you away. That happens sometimes."

Sam and I continue our conversation as we climb into the backseat of Joe's car. He drives slow. *Really* slow. I hope the grocery store isn't too far away. "Maybe. I don't know. When I realized I had feelings for him, it hit me out of nowhere."

"Well, if you ask me, Azrael made a huge mistake. He could've had a really great girl in his life."

I don't think Azrael was looking for *any* girl, let alone, me. Unlike the notorious Jophiel, the Angel of Death really does appear to be celibate.

The store is only a few blocks away, so we reach our destination sooner than I expected. Joe slowly coasts into one of the parking spaces and climbs out of his car.

Sam asks, "So, what kind of friend should we be looking for? What sort of person would fit in Joe's life?"

"I don't know. Anyone who doesn't look scary would be good." I say this as we pass a guy with a pink mohawk and a face full of piercings. "Joe needs someone who seems kind of mellow, like him."

"Old or young?" Sam asks.

"Any of the above." I laugh. "Let's just start throwing a bunch of random people in his path."

While Joe is checking prices of bread loaves, I convince a friendly-looking middle-aged woman to speak to him. By "convince," I mean I screamed the suggestion into her ear.

"Excuse me, do you know if the Sunbeam bread is still on sale? I don't see a tag." It doesn't seem like the sort of question that's going to strike up a friendship, but at least I got her talking.

"I think so," Joe says—then he grabs a loaf of bread and steers his cart away from her.

"Yikes." I grumble to Sam, "This isn't going to be easy, is it?"

"Probably not. This doesn't seem like the greatest place to meet people."

Sam's right, but we keep trying. I lead an old woman, about the same age as Joe, into his aisle. She gives him a long look, but she doesn't say anything. Sam tries to get him talking to a young guy in his twenties, but they don't get past a brief discussion about how chilly the weather is. I convince a teenage store clerk to exchange pleasantries with him, but to be honest, Joe is starting to look somewhat annoyed by all the random conversations. It's put him in a grumpy mood—or maybe he's *always* grumpy and I'm just now realizing it?

I ask Sam, "This isn't going to work, is it?"

"Well... it certainly doesn't look promising."

Joe fills up his cart with stacks of frozen dinners. With his personal mission accomplished, he starts heading toward the checkout lanes. Before he gets there, a little brown-haired girl, about five or six, breaks away from her mom and surprises our charge with a hug.

"Oh my!" Joe exclaims as he's snared by the child's encompassing arms. "And who are you?"

"Ava." Looking up at him, she asks, "Are you old?"

Joe belly laughs at her question. "You could say that."

"Will you be my grandpa?"

Before he can answer Ava's question, her mom rushes over with profuse apologies and a shaking head.

"I am so sorry, sir," the mother says. "Ava's not usually like this. I don't know what's going on with her."

Smiling down at Ava, Joe says, "You don't have to apologize, ma'am. It's been a long time since anyone's hugged me. It was nice."

The lady asks, "What's your name, sir?"

"Joe."

"Well... say goodbye to Mr. Joe, Ava."

Ava shakes her head so fast, her pigtails swat her cheeks. "Nuh uh. I like Mr. Joe. He's going to be my grandpa and my friend."

In the middle of their exchange, Archangel Azrael emerges from one of the aisles. His hands are in his pockets, and there's a smug grin on his face. It's rare to see him crack any kind of smile, even a self-satisfied one.

"Well, Miss Alvarez... what do you think of my choice for Mr. Joe?" Azrael asks. "The little girl wanted a grandpa, he wanted a friend, so it seemed like an obvious match to me."

I'm not too thrilled that he just hijacked our mission, but I can't deny they look cute together, especially when Ava defies her mother to steal another hug from Joe. The old man's laughter and surprise are touching.

"If they can make it work, I guess I approve," I tell him.

It looks like they *will* make it work, because the mother exchanges contact information with Joe. Her daughter insists on it.

"Hello, Sam," Azrael greets my new partner. "I hope you don't mind if I steal Miss Alvarez away from you?"

"*What?*" I squeak. "What does that mean?"

"It means I made a terrible mistake," says Azrael. "I said goodbye to a promising new Helper, and I now realize the error of my ways. If you would like to continue your training, I would love to have you."

For the first few seconds, all I can do is glare at him. He *really* hurt me. He ignored me for such a long time, I don't think I should make it so easy on him.

Sam gives me a nudge and whispers in my ear, "*Do it.* This is what you wanted, isn't it?"

"Alright, *fine.*" I succumb a lot faster than I meant to. At the very least, I should have waited for an apology from him. "But... I don't want to get so caught up in the Helper stuff that I don't have time to go back and check on Joe. I'm not just going to assume Ava's mom will get in contact with him again."

"Fair enough. I will try not to overwhelm you with the *Helper stuff*, as you put it."

I have no idea why Azrael changed his mind, and I don't ask. I'm just glad this is happening, and Sam looks happy for me too. "Alright then. Where does this leave us? Am I officially reinstated?"

"Officially, yes. We will resume your training immediately." Clapping a hand on my shoulder, he adds, "It's good to have you back."

Chapter Twenty: Azrael

A FEW MINUTES AFTER we arrive at our latest charge's side, Lucy is already in tears. Her tendency to get emotional really does make me question her ability to handle the tasks she'll be expected to perform. You can't get personally invested in every death—you just can't. It would drive you insane.

Nevertheless, I'm glad she's with me again. Her smile, full of light, is infectious. Her eyes, her lips, her laugh—I've missed them all. I've even missed her disagreeing with me and nagging me about movies.

Our charge, Eliza Gorman, is a thirteen-year-old girl with an inoperable brain tumor. Her body didn't respond to chemotherapy, and she will likely die before the end of the week. Asylum Sixty-Eight has already made a place for Eliza in preparation for her arrival. Since we're dealing with cancer, I imagine this is a very personal mission for Lucy, but it's Eliza's speech for her mother that reduces my student to tears.

"Mom..." Eliza reaches for her mother's hand and pulls it closer. "Mom... Mom... I love you. I'll always love you. Please don't cry anymore. *Please.* You'll make me cry too."

"I don't want to lose you!" Miranda Gorman can barely bellow the words through her sobs. In her free hand, she's clutching at least three sodden tissues. Damp as they are, they've become ineffective at drying her tears. "You're my best friend. You're my baby. I can't. I *can't.*"

Miranda's head collapses on her daughter's stomach. Eliza strokes her hair until she stops crying.

Eliza says, "I don't want you to be upset anymore, Mom. I'm okay. I'm not scared of dying."

"*I'm* scared!" Miranda cries. "I don't know how I'm supposed to live in a world without my little girl."

"Shh..." Eliza tries to console her with a pat on the head. "Please don't cry anymore. It just makes me sadder."

Eliza once had hair as red as her mother's. She's lost every strand, but the freckles on her face still identify her as a ginger. Her skin is ashen, her cheeks are sunken, and she has the most tired blue eyes I've ever seen. Like many in her place, I think she's ready for her suffering to end. She's ready to find out what awaits after death.

Eliza and her mum were supposed to be watching a movie—one of Eliza's favorites, apparently. When a character died in the film, it triggered her mother's tears, and she's been crying ever since.

"I prayed so hard!" Miranda says, dabbing her cheeks with her soggy bundle of tissues. "I prayed *every* day, hoping for a miracle. I really believed you'd get better. I thought the doctors would figure something out, or there would be divine intervention or... or *something*. If there's a God, I can't believe he'd be cruel enough to let you die before me!"

"Mom..." Eliza tries to be consoling, but her composure is cracking too. "I prayed too. Dad did. Grandma did. I just think... sometimes, people die. People are dying all over the world."

"But why did it have to be *you?*" Miranda asks. "It hurts my heart to see you like this. It hurts my heart to know you're in pain... to know you'll be gone soon. I can't, Eliza. I can't do it anymore."

It almost sounds like she's suicidal. If so, I'll have to add her to my watchlist. In the corner of my eye, I can see Miss Alvarez watching me. I know what's on her mind. She doesn't even have to ask.

"Azrael..."

The first time she utters my name, I pretend I hadn't heard her.

"*Azrael!*"

She said it louder that time, so I guess I have to face her. "Yes?"

"Why can't you give them a miracle?" she asks. "Why can't you just... try?"

Lucy's beautiful, sullen eyes put a chink in my armor. I think I've lost the ability to resist her. "I suppose I could."

Lucy gasps at my reply. "You *could?*"

"Sure. It's been some time since I've asked for a miracle. Eliza seems like a worthy recipient of one." Have I made it too easy on her? Lucy's influence on me is becoming astronomical.

"You're seriously going to try?"

"I am seriously going to try, Miss Alvarez... *Lucy.*" I can feel a rare—albeit tiny—smile on my lips. "You wait here, and I'll address the Council. I would advise you not to get too excited, however. Not every miracle is approved."

I warp back to Archangel Tower and request a Council meeting in the Great Hall. When one of us makes a request, the first five available Archangels assemble for a vote. The speed at which they arrive often depends on the person who makes the request. A lower ranking angel, such as Lucy's friend Sam, might have to wait several hours for five Archangels to answer his summons. When Michael requests an Assembly, *more* than five often arrive within the first thirty seconds. While I don't get my five as quickly as Michael, I'm only waiting for a few minutes.

My Council includes Archangels Raphael, Sandalphon and Haniel, as well as two newer Archangels, Duanphen and Anthony. The latter two have only had Archangel status for a few centuries as opposed to a few millennia. I can usually count on Sandalphon and Haniel to side with me, regardless of my request. The others, however, could be more difficult to convince.

The highest-ranking Archangel usually presides over the meeting. In this case, Archangel Raphael is the highest. He's one of Michael's cronies, and he's a difficult man to impress. Before the Assembly begins, he raises his beak-like nose and glares at me with his small, black eyes.

Raphael's never liked me much, but no matter how much he glares, I'm not intimidated. *I actually outrank* *him*.

When everyone's gathered and seated, Raphael clears his throat and asks, "Archangel Azrael... you've summoned us today because you're requesting a miracle? Do I understand that correctly?"

"You do," I answer, nodding deeply.

Raphael requests, "Can you tell us about the miracle you're requesting, and who will be receiving it?"

I sum up the situation as concisely as I can. "There is a thirteen-year-old child named Eliza Gorman, and the tumor in her head will soon take her life. Eliza and her mother have both made sincere prayers for a miracle. If possible, I would like to dissolve the tumor and restore her to full health."

"Tell us more about Eliza, if you would," Raphael says. "And if the others have any questions, feel free to ask."

"Eliza is a good girl with a gentle aura and a strong capacity for love. She's a straight-A student, a devoted daughter, and I believe she deserves a second chance at life."

Sandalphon asks, "Was this *your* decision... or were you influenced by a certain someone?"

Bastard. Sandalphon won't win me any points by calling attention to this. As one of my closest companions, he knows about my feelings for Lucy, and he knows I took her on another mission today. I almost never ask for miracles, so he must have guessed this was Lucy's idea, not mine.

I explain, "I have been spending time with a Helper trainee, a young lady named Luciana Alvarez. While this miracle was initially her idea, I agreed that it was a good one. The desperate pleas of Eliza's mother were also convincing. I can play them back, if you'd like."

I push a button on my LightTab, replaying Miranda's tearful speech for the Council.

"I prayed every day, hoping for a miracle. I really believed you'd get better. I thought the doctors would figure something out, or there would be divine intervention or... or something. If there's a God, I can't believe he'd be cruel enough to let you die before me."

"She sounds a bit entitled to me," Anthony shares his opinion with a sneer. "She obviously doesn't realize how much energy it takes to perform a miracle of this magnitude."

"I think we should grant it," Duanphen says, so I give her an appreciative nod. I'm glad she's here. Females, for whatever reason, are more inclined to vote *yes*. "Like Anthony said, such a miracle would require a great deal of energy. It would sap most angels, but for Azrael, I imagine it would be easy."

Raphael turns to Haniel and asks, "What is *your* opinion? You've been quiet thus far."

"I agree with Duanphen," Haniel says—and I'm not surprised. I can always count on her support. "It's been a really long time since Azrael's asked for a miracle. If he was throwing around his power and asking for daily miracles, I can see why that might make you pause... but he's not. It doesn't matter if this idea came from Miss Alvarez or Azrael. I think we should grant it."

When Haniel finishes her speech, Raphael asks, "Azrael, is there anything else you would like to add on Eliza's behalf?" I shake my head, so he poses his next question to the Council. "Does anyone else have something to say?"

I hold my breath and keep an eye on Anthony. He's been my greatest challenger so far, but he doesn't say anything. I only need a majority vote: three out of five. The ladies will side with me, and unless Sandalphon decides to stab me in the back, he should be the final vote I need.

One by one, the Archangels cast their votes, and when the results are revealed, I'm shocked.

It was unanimous. All five Archangels granted my request.

Eliza—and Lucy—will be getting the miracle they wanted.

Chapter Twenty-One: Luciana

"Well, Lucy, you got your miracle."

I throw my arms around Azrael when he delivers the good news. It might not be appropriate to ambush the Angel of Death with a hug, but I can't stop myself. I've always wanted to witness a miracle, and Eliza deserves one.

Sadly, our hug is one-sided. His arms never embrace me.

"Was it hard to get it approved?" I ask.

"Surprisingly, no. It was a unanimous vote. Don't start getting ideas, however. It will be a long time before I pester the Council for another miracle."

Azrael's lustrous wings unfurl and stretch as he steps out of my hug. He approaches Eliza's bed, kneels, and wraps the feathery appendages around her. For a moment, Azrael and Eliza are surrounded in staggering bright light, and even though I'm not standing that close, I can feel the light's warmth. Eliza's in the middle of a nap, totally unconscious, but her body twitches as he takes her tumor.

"And that should be it," Azrael says. "The next time she wakes, she'll be well again, and her recovery will baffle everyone who examines her."

When Azrael stumbles, I ask, "Are you okay?"

"Yes. It's just a bit draining. In fact, I'll probably need to rest for a day or two."

"Really?" I wince at his answer. "I didn't know it would be so hard on you."

"It won't be so bad. A lesser angel would need an entire week of rest after a miracle like that. I'm sorry if that sounds arrogant, but it's true. It's—"

Azrael is interrupted by a scream from Miranda. She's in the kitchen, so I hurry from Eliza's bedroom to check on her. The cause of her panic is an adorable home invader: a little white dove. He's on the kitchen counter, watching her with a cocked head and blinking black eyes. Miranda keeps trying to shoo him through the open window, to no avail.

"Go! Get out of here!" Miranda waves an arm to encourage the bird's departure, but he stubbornly sticks to her counter. "*Please* leave! Ugh!"

"I sent the bird to her," Azrael reveals as he follows me into the kitchen. "The bird's supposed to be a messenger, to let her know her miracle's been granted. Unfortunately, humans are often blind to the signs we show them."

Miranda whimpers at the bird, "Please go! You're not supposed to be here!" After a final coo, the dove takes off through the window.

I point out the obvious, as I often do. "I think the bird scared her."

"Well, she shouldn't have been scared. The bird was very much on her team." Azrael holds out an elbow and asks, "Are you ready to go? As I said, I'll be taking a break for a day or so. When I've recovered my lost energy, we can return and check on Eliza."

I take his arm and warp us back to Archangel Tower. I want him to know I've been practicing my warping, but he doesn't look impressed. In fact, he looks tired. *Really* tired. A part of me feels guilty for having begged for a miracle.

"Will you be okay?" I ask.

"Of course. You should note, however, that it's difficult to bring someone back from the brink of death. Without question, Eliza would have died without our intervention."

"Well, I appreciate what you did, and I'm sorry you have to suffer the effects of it," I tell him. "I'll, uh... I guess I'll see you in a couple of days?"

"Indeed." Azrael steps backward, toward the Tower's entrance. His hand is cupped over his face, which makes me wonder if he's trying to hide from his fans at the gate. "I'll be in contact with you shortly."

He hurries into the Tower before any fangirls can spot him and scream his name.

WHEN AZRAEL DOESN'T contact me for the next two days, I start to get concerned. Am I fired again? Is he ill? What's going on? I texted him once *and* only once, asking how he is, and when he never wrote back, I was too proud to text again.

Azrael seems *really* bad at answering his texts. What a crappy, inattentive boyfriend he would be.

I'm glad he gave Eliza her miracle, though, and I *am* worried about him. He, on the other hand, probably hasn't given me a second thought. I warp to Archangel Tower, where I'm greeted by a seven-foot-tall angel with slate gray wings. I have no idea if I'm allowed to enter again, but it's worth a shot.

"Hi. I'm Lucy Alvarez," I introduce myself. "I'm here to check on—"

"Azrael," the gate guard finishes. "He's in the garden. You're permitted to enter, but don't wander too much."

The guard lets me beyond the gate and points me in the direction of the garden, where rainbow flowers line a cobbled path. I pass several manicured topiaries that have been sculpted to look like the Archangels, including Azrael. In fact, his hedge is the tallest one of all.

Suddenly, a voice asks, "Are you looking for Azrael?"

I whirl around, totally oblivious to the fact that someone was standing behind me. Actually, there are two people. Archangel Jophiel is in a wicker gazebo with a girl who looks about the same age as me.

"Uh... yeah," I reply. "Do you know where he is?"

"I think I saw him sulking in that general direction," Jophiel says, thrusting a thumb over his shoulder. "Look for a gold fountain. He's in that area."

"Okay, thanks." For a moment, I watch the young woman next to Jophiel. Everyone heard the story about his arrest, his trial, and the girl who stole his heart. I wonder if this is her? "Are you... Anna?"

Chuckling, she says, "Yes, I'm Anna. I'm always surprised when people know my name. That's what I get for dating an Archangel, I guess."

Since I'm halfway in love with an Archangel myself, I would love to pick her brain on this topic, but I don't want to bother them. I say goodbye, thank them for the information, and follow Jophiel's directions. Within a minute, I locate the gold fountain he talked about. It's hard to miss. It's a giant golden hand with silver water burbling in the palm. It's kind of weird, but mesmerizing, so I stand and watch it for a few minutes.

While I'm transfixed by the fountain, Azrael finds me and stands at my side. "Hello, Lucy," he greets me. "I didn't expect to find you wandering around the garden. What brings you here?"

"*You*," I reply. "When you didn't respond to my text, I got worried, so I went looking for you."

"Sorry. I wasn't avoiding you. I turned off my LightTab," Azrael says. "If I had it on, I would have been tempted to take missions, but I know I need to rest. I can't go around slaying demons in the state I'm in."

"Is it still bad?" I ask.

"No. I've mostly recovered. In another day or so, I should be able to get back to work." Azrael's lip curls as he studies the golden fountain.

"This is such an eyesore, isn't it? I can think of million shapes that would be more aesthetically pleasing than a giant hand."

"I dunno." I shrug. "I kinda like it."

"You and Michael both. As long as he likes it, the damn thing's not going anywhere." Azrael abruptly changes the subject. "So... I'm actually glad you're here. Eliza had her first doctor's appointment since her miracle, so I thought we'd check on her... if you're willing to accompany me?"

"Of course! Why wouldn't I be willing?"

I wish there was some way to properly thank him for helping Eliza. My first hug wasn't well-received, so I doubt he'd respond well to another one. The "Angel of Death" is about as affectionate as his title would suggest.

Azrael warps us directly to Eliza's visit with the doctor. Miranda's at her side, tearfully absorbing the doctor's report.

"I've never seen anything like it," the doctor says. "There's no evidence of any tumor in her brain. It's as if it was never there. Her blood count's stabilized, and her organs appear to be functioning normally. I hesitate to use the word *miracle*, but... Eliza's current condition is truly inexplicable."

Miranda and Eliza are both crying again. This time, though, I imagine they're tears of relief. I glance at Azrael, noticing he looks paler than usual. He said he's mostly recovered, but I don't know if I believe him. Now I know why angels are hesitant to grant miracles.

"That's not the reason we're hesitant." Azrael answers the thought in my head—which I hate. How often does he listen to my thoughts?

"Not often, honestly," Azrael replies, even though he's doing it *again*. "I turn off my telepathic powers as much as I can. Anyway... we usually don't grant miracles because we prefer not to choose one human over another. At least, that's *my* reason. I can't speak for everyone."

When the doctor exits, Eliza and her mother embrace and cry in each other's arms. Seeing how happy they are, I have to smile. Azrael can object all he wants, but I think that miracle was a good call. I feel bad that it drained him, but I'm glad Eliza's okay.

"There's nothing to stop her from having a long life, free from cancer," Azrael says. "You should be proud of yourself."

"*You* should be proud of yourself," I correct him. "You're the one who performed the miracle and made it happen."

"No. *You* did." Leaning closer to my ear, Azrael whispers, "I only did it because I wanted to make you happy."

Chapter Twenty-Two: Luciana

AZRAEL WANTS TO MAKE me happy. I've been trying to process that thought for several hours now, but it's like my mind cannot compute. Does that mean he likes me? Am I reading too much into it?

I spill all the details to Sam, even though I'm sure he's sick of hearing about my adventures with Azrael.

"He actually said the words, *I want to make you happy*?" Sam asks.

"Yes. He *actually* said those words."

We're standing outside of Asylum Seventeen, just after the playground's emptied out for the day. If Sam's not interested in my Azrael drama, he's doing a good job faking it.

"How did he say it?" Sam asks. "Was his voice husky... or serious, or...?"

I reply quickly, "Serious. Azrael's always serious."

"Hmm." Sam drags a hand through his golden blonde hair as he ruminates. "If he actually said those words, it really does sound like he likes you."

"I know, right? So... what should I do about it?"

"Does he have any idea you like him?" Sam asks.

"If he's been listening to my thoughts for even a fraction of a second, which I *know* he does, then it should be obvious to him."

"No, that's not good enough," Sam protests. "Maybe he's waiting for you to tell him? With words."

Shy as I am, I can't imagine standing in front of Archangel Azrael and telling him I have feelings for him. There's *no way* that would happen. Plus, I'm still paranoid about the fact that he fired me once.

What if my confession would make him fire me again? "Is there any way I can show him without... y'know... outright telling him?" I ask.

"You need to spend some time with him away from your Helper work," Sam advises me. "You said he's been unwell lately, right?"

"Yeah. He's sick because of me. I asked him to perform a miracle, and when he did, it drained him."

Sam strokes his chin and plots on my behalf. "Perhaps you could show up at his office with a bowl of chicken noodle soup or something?"

Sam's suggestion makes me giggle. Chicken soup is good for a cold, but I doubt it would have any effect on whatever is ailing Azrael.

"Don't laugh!" Sam exclaims. "It's the thought that counts. You're letting him know you care."

"Maybe I could make it like a movie date? I can show up with the soup, manifest a pizza, and cozy up to him on the couch."

"Maybeee..." The hesitation in Sam's voice says he's not quite sold on my plan. "Is there any way you can make it obvious that you're showing up for a date?"

"Apart from saying, *this is a date*? I dunno." I throw up a shoulder and sigh through the corner of my mouth. I have no experience when it comes to stuff like this. If Azrael really *does* like me—which I doubt—I wish he would make the first move.

"Maybe that's what you should do? Be direct with him," Sam suggests. "Anyway, I should probably get back to the kids. Send me an update if there are any new developments."

We part with a hug, and on my way home, I start reading articles on my LightTab. *How to Snag Your Man* and *How to Get Him To Like You* aren't very enlightening, *Five Easy Ways to Make Him Swoon* seems helpful, though. According to this, men are visual creatures with short attention spans, and a sexy red dress can catch their attention. Maybe that's what I need? I need a sexy dress and a hairstyle change?

I hurry back home, breeze past my mom, and enter my room for privacy. I manifest the wavy locks of a Victoria's Secret model, a red v-neck dress, and matching lipstick to go with it. I don't really look like myself, but I think I look pretty good. One of those articles said *don't change yourself*, but maybe a slight change is needed to push him in the right direction?

Even though I think it's kind of silly, I follow Sam's advice and manifest a bowl of chicken soup. When I'm ready, I warp to Azrael's location and appear in front of Archangel Tower. The guards are starting to recognize me, and to my surprise, they let me in right away.

Azrael's office door opens as soon as I arrive. The Angel of Death is standing on the other side in a white tank top and black pants. He leans against the door frame, crosses his arms, and asks, "What's with the dress?"

"Huh. You don't like it?"

"No, it's fine. I'm just wondering if there's a cocktail party I wasn't invited to." When his remark gets no reaction from me, he adds, "I'm teasing, Lucy."

Ack, he's such a disappointment! *Fine* is not the compliment I was hoping for. *Fine* is pitiful. I wanted him to think I look pretty, but instead, he's making smart ass remarks about my dress. Never have I been more tempted to wring a guy's neck.

"You can come in, if you want," Azrael says, stepping out of the doorway. "I'm just working on some paperwork while I recover. I should be ready to take new missions tomorrow."

Gliding into the room, I raise my bowl of soup and announce, "I brought you something!"

"Oh?" He raises an eyebrow and waits for me to elaborate.

"Yeah. It's chicken soup. I thought it might help with your... illness?" There was probably a better word than *illness*, but I couldn't think of one. "And, uh... I know you could just manifest a bowl for yourself if you wanted to, but this is my mom's recipe. It's the best chicken noodle soup in the world, I swear."

"Thank you." As he accepts the bowl from my outstretched hands, he adds, "I'm not really ill, though."

"I know. Angels can't get ill. What word should I have used? Fatigued?"

"Not really," Azrael says. "It's more like... a need to recharge. Nevertheless, thank you for the soup. It's a sweet gesture."

"So, uh..." I slide across the floor, closer to Azrael. "I was wondering if you wanted to watch another movie?"

His hollow reply gives me no hope. "Seriously?"

"Yeah. Sure. Why not? You're not going on any missions right now, so there's no better time to watch one!"

"I might not be going on missions, but that doesn't mean I don't have a ton of work to do," he says, pointing at the growing stack of papers on his desk.

"Why would an Archangel have so much paperwork?" I ask.

"Because there's a surprising lot of work that goes into running this place."

At this point, I want to slink through the door and warp back home. He doesn't look happy to see me, he didn't like my dress, and now he doesn't want to watch a movie. I'm probably a fool for thinking he could ever like me. I wish Sam would've hit me with a dose of reality instead of encouraging me to do this.

Suddenly, Azrael asks, "Alright... what movie did you have in mind?"

"That depends. What genre are you interested in?" Feeling a bit more confident, I sit down on his couch and smooth my hands over my dress. The television I manifested last time is still in Azrael's office—I'm surprised he didn't get rid of it. "Horror? Comedy? Drama?"

"Any of the above... although, honestly, horror would be my last choice. I'll never understand why humans like to scare themselves."

Azrael joins me on the couch, albeit on the opposite end of it. I wish he would've sat a bit closer, but I'll take what I can get.

I manifest a big bowl of cheese popcorn and put it between us. "Let's watch *Thor*. I was obsessed with that movie when I was a kid. I think I watched it about thirty times. The guy who plays Thor was my first crush... I must've been ten or eleven. To be honest, he kind of reminds me of Archangel Michael."

"Does that mean you have a crush on Archangel Michael?" Azrael asks.

"*Nooo!*" I squeal. "No no no... I did *not* mean to make it sound like that!"

"You don't have to be ashamed of your crush, Lucy. *Everyone* has a crush on Archangel Michael." Azrael helps himself to a fistful of my popcorn. Before he munches on it, I catch a glimpse of a grin on his lips. Is he teasing me again?

"Well, *I* don't," I insist. "After awhile, my interests changed. I started to prefer guys with dark hair and dark eyes instead." Azrael's got one dark eye and one blue eye, but the description fits him well enough.

"Oh?"

"Uh huh." I turn on *Thor* and pitch a few pieces of popcorn in my mouth. Boldly, I ask, "What's Archangel Azrael's type?"

"Nice girls, smart girls, compassionate girls," Azrael replies. "Physically, I don't really have a preference."

His answer is kind of deflating. I was hoping he would describe someone who looked like me.

"But..." Azrael spreads an arm across the back of the couch and continues, "I've been alone for a long time. I haven't spent a lot of time thinking about the sort of girl I'd be interested in."

I stop talking and focus on Thor. Thor makes me happy. Unlike Azrael, Thor never disappoints.

When we're several minutes in, Azrael points at the screen and says, "He's got a giant hammer to match his giant ego. For that reason alone, he really *does* remind me of Michael."

I replenish our popcorn and whine, "Hey, don't insult Thor! He's my favorite comic book hero ever."

During the movie, Azrael is surprisingly pleasant company. He indulges me in conversations about Loki, Heimdall's badass sword (which reminds me of Azrael's), and lady warriors. I've always admired kick ass women.

"I should let you sit in on an Archangel training session sometime," Azrael says. "There's no one who kicks more ass than—"

I never find out who kicks ass, because a beep from Azrael's LightTab steals his attention.

"Hey, I thought you had that turned off!" I exclaim.

"I did. I turned it on this morning." Rising from the couch, he says, "Lucy... we have to go."

We're nearing the end of the movie, and now I doubt we'll ever finish it. "What? Why?"

"I just got a message about Paul," Azrael says. "He's in the hospital, and he's running out of time."

Chapter Twenty-Three: Luciana

PAUL IS SURROUNDED by his three daughters, and there isn't a dry eye among them. He's awake but barely coherent, and his hospital food hasn't been touched. The eldest daughter, Dawn, tries to feed him applesauce, but he spits it out and shoots a sour face in her direction. His youngest daughter, Carmen, is the one we encountered before. She looks way too young to be an orphan, but she's going to be one soon.

Paul's kidneys are failing rapidly, and dialysis hasn't produced any results. It's only a matter of time before Azrael and I have to take him Home.

When the daughters step out to get food, Azrael says, "I told you I would help with his memory loss... so that's what I'm going to do. He's weak, so I'll have to give him energy first, then I'll try to unravel his mind."

"Are you sure you're well enough to do that? I thought you were still trying to recuperate."

"I should be fine."

I clothesline Azrael with an arm before he reaches the bed. "Wait. Maybe *I* could give him an energy boost? I've never done it before, but I've read about the technique."

"You can try," Azrael says. "But if you can't do it, I'll have to step in."

"Give me a chance! If I become a Helper, won't I have to do things like this all the time?" Whether it's an advanced technique or not, I'd like to try. I shuffle closer to Paul's bed and place a hand on his forehead. According to what I've read, you need to focus on loving thoughts—so *of course* my mind jumps to Azrael. Right now he's posing

118

like a model, with one hand dragging through his hair and the other hand stuffed in a pocket. When he looks as hot as this, the loving thoughts just pour into my head. Energy-infused chills scurry through my body and flood into Paul.

"Well done, Lucy," Azrael praises me. "I could feel an immediate shift in him. It tells me you've succeeded."

Paul's eyes snap open and focus on my face, so I tell him, "Hi! I'm Luciana. I'm one of your spirit guides. The guy over there is an angel. We're going to take care of you while you're in the hospital, okay?"

I have no idea if he can hear or see me, but Azrael always says our comforting words can have a positive effect on our charges. I give Paul a smile and a light squeeze on the shoulder.

I continue, "Your daughters love you a lot. I can tell. You're a lucky man to have the love of so many girls!"

Paul opens his dry lips and tries to say something, but his mumbles are impossible to decipher.

"I'll try to restore his mind now," Azrael says. "I can't guarantee I'll be able to do it, but I do have a rather high success rate."

Like me, Azrael puts a hand on Paul's head. Unlike me, Azrael has light trickling from his fingertips. The luminous ribbons flood into our charge's scalp, and it must feel good, because Paul has a big, dopey grin on his lips.

"He seemed to like that," I point out.

"Perhaps. He probably felt a pleasant tingling sensation as I attempted to awaken the damaged parts of his brain," Azrael explains. "It should only take a few minutes to kick in. When his daughters return, they'll be surprised by how alert he is."

Dawn, Carmen and Ada are gone for less than an hour, and they return with a hot fudge sundae. Paul stretches out an arm and says, "I was wondering when you girls would get here. Ooh, gimme that thing!"

All three daughters look stunned. When they left, their father could barely open his eyes, eat, or lift a finger. Now he's sitting up in bed, reaching for a snack.

"Dad..." Carmen tiptoes to his bed with hesitation in her steps, as if she's approaching a stranger. "Dad, do you know who we are?"

"Of course I know who you are! What kind of question is that?"

As soon as the sundae is in his hands, he picks up a spoon and starts shoveling ice cream into his mouth. I think I'm as stunned as his daughters are. The last time I saw him, he barely knew how to hold a fork. Azrael claims he didn't perform a miracle, but it has to be close.

"I'm giving them one last day with him," Azrael says. "They get one last day with the father they used to know... and then he'll be gone."

"No one's ever really *gone*, though." I correct him in a stern voice that would make Amber proud. Those were the first words she said to me after she took me Home. *No one's really gone.*

"True enough... but they will certainly feel his absence," Azrael says. "When someone passes on to the next world, it can leave a gaping void, as you well know."

Paul identifies all of his daughters, one by one. *Ada. Carmen. Dawn.* They're so impressed by his improved memory, a couple of them are in tears. I feel bad for them, though. They might think their father is getting better, but their hope will be short-lived.

Carmen pulls a laptop out of a messenger bag and fires up a video on the hospital wifi. It's an episode of *The Three Stooges.* Those guys must be popular with his generation, because my granddad watched them too. Paul brightens up even more at the sight of Larry, Curly and Moe. He even does an impression of Curly, filled with whoops and nyuks.

I ask Azrael, "So... when Paul passes away, his dementia will just be gone, right?"

"Absolutely. A spirit body isn't attached to the processes of a brain. He'll be free of the parts that are causing his confusion. He still has a bit more time with his daughters, but we should probably check on him tomorrow."

All of this talk about dads and death is making me miss *my* papá, so I ask Azrael, "Would it be alright if I went to visit my dad and brother?"

"Of course," Azrael says. "Would it be alright if I went with you?"

His question stuns me for a moment. It's a good kind of stunned, like when you get a better grade than you expected, or when you get exactly what you wanted for your birthday. If Azrael is interested in seeing my family, that can only be a good sign—right?

My reply comes after a brief delay. "Uh, sure. I would like it if you came. I'll try to hold back my tears. The first time I saw them, and they couldn't see me, it hit me hard. I was ugly crying the entire time."

I grab Azrael's arm and take him to my dad's place: a squat, square house on the corner of a busy street. It's as ordinary as a house can get, and it probably needs some renovations, but it was my home. I miss it.

We find my dad in the yard, pruning the overgrown hedges. I approach him with a pouty lip and hover a few feet behind him.

"This is your dad, I take it?" Azrael asks.

"Yep. This is Papá." My hand passes through him when I try to touch his shoulder. I know he can't feel me, or even hear me, but I tell him anyway, "I miss you, Papá. I just want you to know that Mom and I are okay. We wish we could be with you, but... all we can really do right now is watch over you from a distance."

I continue my speech while holding back tears. "Grandma and Grandpa are okay too. I know they wish they could be with you... just like I do. I wish I could hug you. I know you didn't really like hugs, but if you could see me right now, I'd give you a big one anyway. You would just have to deal with it."

"Are you okay?" Azrael asks. I know he can see the twinkling gloss in my eyes. Not a single tear has fallen yet, but seeing my dad has been challenging.

"Yeah. I'm okay. Let's head into the house and find Luis."

Luis is four years older than me. He just graduated from college and moved back home after I died. He probably thought Dad needed a companion. We find him upstairs, in his old room, strumming his guitar. I sit on the end of his bed and listen for awhile. When he finishes his song, I reward him with unheard applause.

"I always did like your music," I tell him. "You're super talented, I just wish you could get over your stage fright."

"His permanent spirit guide has been trying to help him with that," Azrael says, looking at his LightTab. "Your brother wants to be famous, but it's not going to happen if he doesn't put himself out there."

"Yeah. I can't blame him for being nervous, though. I think Luis is an awesome singer and songwriter and he deserves all the praise, but... people can be cruel. When you put yourself out there, you run the risk of some d-bag trashing you on social media."

"A *d-bag*, huh?" Azrael repeats the word with a chuckle. "Are you thinking of anyone in particular?"

"Yeah. There was this one guy... his username was literally notaniceguy7. He posted videos of one of Luis' weaker performances and all the commenters were *so* mean. Luis stopped performing live after that." I pat my brother's knee and give him an encouraging smile, even though I'm sure it has no effect on him. "I miss you, big brother. I want you to know, I'm *always* proud of you, and I think you're a kick ass musician. Congrats on finishing college! If I ever have a break, I'll come here and help you find a job. I know you need one."

"You really care about your family, don't you?" Azrael asks.

"Totally. To me, they're the most important thing in the world. My mom, my dad... everyone. I look forward to the day when we're all reunited, whenever that day may come."

"In a way, I envy you," Azrael says. "I wish I had a family."

"Aren't the Archangels sort of like a family to each other?" I ask.

"No, not really." Azrael heaves a raspy sigh, and his downcast eyes make me wish I was brave enough to hug him. It wouldn't be the first time I hugged him, but the last time was an impulse.

"*I* could be your family." That sounded *way* too intimate, so I follow up with, "Or... you know... the Helpers could be like your family."

"That's kind of you, Lucy," Azrael says. "You're a good girl."

I give my brother a hug, but I can't really hold him too tight because my arms would go through him. He starts playing another song on his guitar, and I'm tempted to stay and listen, but I think I've had enough sadness for one day.

Blinking back tears, I turn to Azrael and say, "Alright... let's go Home."

Chapter Twenty-Four: Luciana

EARLY THE NEXT MORNING, I get an unexpected text from Azrael.

Paul is dying today. I want you to take him Home, and I want you to do it by yourself. Please note, I will be able to hear every word you say. Consider this a test.

I'm a little stunned that he's not going to finish this mission with me. Azrael and I had been visiting Paul together all along, so why would he bail on me now? Even though I knew I would eventually be going on missions by myself, it's a little jarring. What if our last mission together has already come and gone?

I warp to Paul's location. He's been moved to hospice, and by the looks of it, he's not going to be there too long. He's completely unconscious, pale, and bloated. Every now and then, he shudders, which makes me wonder if he's in pain. If he is, couldn't Azrael take his pain away? Ugh, I wish he was here!

All of Paul's daughters are with him again, holding his hands and whispering their final words to him. With tears dripping down her nose, Carmen says, "Mom will be here soon. I just know it."

Oh, that's right! If Paul's dying today, isn't it my job to summon his wife? I turn on my LightTab and search for Cathy Cisternino. There are a few matches, but I easily find the one who's related to Paul and send her a message.

Your husband is dying soon. Please come when you can.

Cathy receives my message and warps to Paul's bedside less than a minute later.

"Hello, dear," she greets me. "Thanks for the message. You... You're not my husband's usual guide."

"No, I'm not. I'm Lucy, one of Azrael's Helpers." I offer her a hand, which she shakes with a smile. I think it's a little weird to see her smiling while her husband's dying, but maybe she's happy they'll be together again?

"Well, it's good to meet you," Cathy says. "I'm afraid you're not seeing me at my best. I was with my daughters a few hours ago, and they kept making me cry. My eyes are still red and puffy."

"Oh, so... you didn't need me to send you a message? You already knew he was dying today?"

"I did know, but I still appreciate the message." Cathy stands behind her youngest daughter, strokes her hair and says, "Poor Carmen. She's going to be such a mess without her father. They lived together after I died. In the later years, he drove her crazy with his dementia, but they were close. They were always close."

"It sucks to lose a parent." That sentence needed more emphasis, so I add, "*Really* sucks."

"Indeed it does," Cathy agrees. "So, what's it like to be one of Azrael's Helpers? I've always envied you guys for getting to work so closely with an Archangel. He's handsome, isn't he?"

Azrael said he would be listening to every word of this. Knowing that, how am I supposed to answer? It would be embarrassing to agree and cruel to disagree. "Umm... yeah. I guess so."

"You guess so? Pfft!" Cathy sputters at my watered down answer. "You *know* he's handsome. Everyone thinks so. A lot of the Archangels are handsome, aren't they? So was my Paul, back in the day. He's still handsome to me, but..." Her fingers trace the faint lines along his forehead.

"He doesn't have too many wrinkles for his age, though. That was one of the first things I thought when I saw him."

"True... true," Cathy agrees. "He wore his age a lot better than I did, that's for sure."

Paul makes a hissing sound that reminds me of a creature in a zombie movie. It's not a pleasant sound, so I ask Cathy, "Do you think he's in pain?"

"I don't know. Maybe? They gave him morphine earlier, but maybe it wasn't enough?"

I go into the hall and shout at one of the nurses to give him more morphine. A self-satisfied smile tugs at my lips when she responds to my command. It's weird to have that effect on people. You have a huge amount of influence on mortals, and they never know you're there.

Soon after Paul gets his morphine, the daughters decide to leave. Tears rain all over him as all three girls lean down to hug him.

It will be the last time they hug him, I'm sure.

"Death's so heartbreaking," I lament.

Cathy says, "Yeah. I wouldn't want your job."

"At one point, *I* didn't even want my job!" I tell her. "Once, Azrael almost dismissed me, and it made me realize how much I wanted it."

I hope Azrael hears that. I want him to know I'm committed to this.

How long is Paul going to fight for his life? Azrael said he was stubborn, so it could be hours. I lean over his ear and whisper a speech that may or may not help him. Azrael seems to think it helps, so I give it a shot. "Hey... I know you might be scared, but there's nothing to be afraid of. Your wife's here, and she's excited to see you again. I know how weird it is to leave your body behind. It's natural to try to resist, but... you just need to let go. Your daughters will be okay. I'll make sure to check on them every now and then, okay?"

About three minutes later, Paul wheezes one last time—then he's standing over his body with shock in his eyes.

"Hello!" I greet him. "I'm Luciana, one of your spirit guides. And I don't think the lovely lady beside me needs an introduction."

A sob explodes from the depths of Paul's belly as he runs to his wife, and when she starts crying, I cry too.

"My baby... my angel," Paul whispers, caressing her cheeks. "I never thought I'd get to see you again."

"I know," Cathy says. "It was your biggest fear."

"And now you're here." Paul wraps his arms around her and starts rocking her back and forth. "My girl. My only girl."

Paul and Cathy almost look like they're dancing, so I turn on my LightTab and start playing *In the Still of the Night*—which, according to Azrael, was a special song to them. For some reason, I'm totally touched by their reunion. I wipe my eyes, blow my nose, and breathe a sigh of relief. The relieved sigh is for Azrael, because I'm glad he isn't here. I wouldn't want him to see me looking like a hot mess.

I wish I could be loved the way Paul loves Cathy. I want a love that stands the test of time, that even death couldn't conquer. I want to be totally, completely, utterly loved. I envy these two.

When the song's over, I say, "So... I'm here to take you Home, to the world where spirits reside. I'm sure you'll be staying with Cathy, so you won't have to worry about living arrangements. If you have any questions, I would be happy to answer them for you."

"Will I ever get to see my daughters again?" Paul asks.

"That's a really good question. We usually don't allow those kinds of visits until you've completed at least one mission."

Paul's eyebrows jump to his forehead. "Mission?"

"Spirit guide missions," I explain. "That might be your biggest surprise of the day. You'll be attending spirit school soon. It's sort of required, but don't worry... it's fulfilling work."

Paul seems to be out of questions, so I warp him back Home and drop them off at Cathy's house. When I'm alone, I type a message to Azrael.

Well... it's over. Did I pass?

I aggressively nibble on my lip until I get a reply.

With flying colors. I'm proud of you, Lucy. I think you'll be able to start taking missions on your own soon.

Azrael's answer is bittersweet. I want to be good at my job, but I want to keep working with him. I have so many mixed feelings, it's making my head hurt.

Dios mio, Lucy, why did you have to fall for an Archangel?

Chapter Twenty-Five: Luciana

"SO, HOW DID IT GO WITH you and Azrael?" Sam asks. "Are the two of you getting married yet, or are you going to need a little more prodding from me?"

Sam wanted to check on Joe Cotton and his new friend, so of course I decided to join him. I love to check on my old charges to make sure they're doing well. I was hoping to avoid the Azrael discussion, but it's the first thing out of Sam's mouth.

"Married?" My lips sputter at the thought. "Trust me, that's never going to happen."

"Why not? You've already given up?"

"I haven't really given up. It's more like... I never even tried," I confess. "He's never going to ask me out, and there's no way I'd ever ask him out, so it's basically a lost cause. Besides, my time with him is almost at an end. He's basically said so himself."

"That's sad. You know, I genuinely thought you had a shot with him. You would've been the envy of a lot of girls if you actually had Archangel Azrael as a boyfriend."

I need to change the subject, fast. I feel silly for ever liking him. Azrael was never going to end a decades-long period of celibacy for someone as unremarkable as me. "So... how are you and Kaleb?" I ask.

"Oh, we're fine. It's the same old same old. He's been asking to have you over for lunch again."

In the middle of his reply, Sam warps us to Joe Cotton's location. We're suddenly standing outside of an unfamiliar house with a tidy lawn and garden. I check my LightTab for an update on our whereabouts. We're in Ohio, it's November 22nd, and there's a thin layer of snowflakes peppering the ground. It seems a little early in the year for snow, but I could be wrong. How's a girl from LA supposed to know anything about snow?

Actually, this is the first time I've seen snow outside of a television, so it's pretty exciting. I stick out my tongue and try to catch one of the falling flakes in my mouth. I'm immune to the coldness of it, but it does feel wet.

"Are you enjoying yourself?" Sam asks.

"I am. I have literally *never* seen snow until this moment." Pointing at the house, I ask, "Who lives here?"

"I have a guess, but... let's go inside and find out."

Sam and I pass through the front door, which is still a little weird to me. As soon as we enter, we find Joe and Ava sitting on the couch. She's built a fort of stuffed animals around him, and he looks delighted by it.

Clapping a hand to my chest, I cry, "Aww, look! They're still friends!"

"So it would seem," Sam says. "Azrael stole that mission from us, but I have to say, he's a pretty good matchmaker."

A giggle slips out of my mouth as Ava bounces one of her stuffed animals—a stuffed tiger—across Joe's lap. Another man, probably Ava's father, says, "Ava... maybe you should stop pestering Mr. Joe?"

"Don't worry. She's not pestering me at all," Joe defends her. "I'm really impressed by all these dolls. She's got quite a collection."

As the bouncy tiger hops along her new friend's arm, Ava asks, "Which one is your favorite, Mr. Joe?"

"You know, I don't think I could pick a favorite. They're all so nice."

Ava gives Joe a hug, leans back, and hugs him again. She's an affectionate little girl, and Joe doesn't seem to mind. He gives her a pat on the head and a smile that doesn't want to fade.

A savory aroma leads me into the kitchen, where Ava's mom is carving one of the most beautiful golden brown turkeys I've ever seen. That's when I realize they've invited him over for Thanksgiving. All the components of a typical American feast are here: mashed potatoes, stuffing, gravy, pie, and green beans. It all looks so delicious, I fantasize about manifesting a Thanksgiving banquet for Sam and me.

"Sam, *look!*" I call him into the kitchen with a squeal. "Look... they've invited him over for Thanksgiving! Isn't that the sweetest thing ever?"

Appearing in the doorway, he agrees, "It *is* pretty sweet. He would probably be making one of his frozen dinners otherwise."

Ava's mother—who the LightTab identifies as *Christine*—prepared this huge feast for just the four of them. As they gather around the dinner table, she playfully refers to Joe as their honored guest.

"That's awfully nice of you, ma'am, but I'm the one who feels honored to be here," Joe says. "I really ought to thank you. Until I met you all, I couldn't think of a single good reason to wake up in the morning."

"And now you have a reason?" Christine asks.

"Well, of course." He reaches over to ruffle Ava's hair. This little girl has really taken to him. She refused to sit in any seat that wasn't next to her new grandpa.

Ava's father says, "You'll have to come for Christmas too... if that's not assuming too much?"

"Believe me, I would love to come over for Christmas. But I wouldn't want to take advantage of your hospitality."

Christine swats his arm and chastises him, "Are you serious? I think Ava would be upset if you didn't come for Christmas. Unless... did you have somewhere else you need to be?"

"No, ma'am. I haven't had a place to be for several years now," Joe admits as his fork plunges into tender turkey. "I can't thank you enough for all of this. I really can't."

I wanted to stay and salivate over their Thanksgiving dinner, but a message on my LightTab captures my attention from their feast. It's from Azrael.

Look out the window.

"That's weird." I thought I was whispering to myself, but I guess Sam overheard me.

"What's weird?" he asks.

"This text. It's from Azrael." I flash him a glimpse of the mysterious text on my LightTab. "Hang on, I'll be right back."

I go to the nearest window, but when I try to peel back the curtain, it doesn't budge. I keep forgetting how difficult it is to effect anything in the physical world. With a shrug, I stick my head *through* the curtain and peer outside.

Azrael is standing outside with a bundle of flowers in his hand. His black coat and black hair are covered in snowflakes, and I am *really* confused right now. My eyes stick to the flowers as I head out to greet him.

"Azrael," I whisper his name. "What are you doing here?"

"I'm here to see you... and to check on Joe Cotton. I'm disappointed you didn't invite me too. Was I not a major part of that mission?"

"Yeah. Sorry. I guess I didn't think you'd be interested." My stomach is a bundle of nerves right now. I don't think I've felt this nervous since I've been dead.

"*Of course* I'm interested. Does Joe still have his little friend?"

"Yeah. She really adores him too."

"Good." Azrael's lips are bent by a rare smile as he holds out the flowers. "These are for you, Lucy."

"Flow...ers," I stupidly mumble the word. "Uh, why are you giving me flowers?"

I couldn't have been less prepared for his answer.

"Because I like you." Azrael's smile turns a bit cheeky as he studies my reaction. "It's been a long time since I've said this to anyone, but... would you consider going on a date with me?"

Chapter Twenty-Six: Azrael

LUCY LOOKS SO SHOCKED by my request, you would think I asked her to reincarnate as a sea urchin. Is her reaction a good or bad sign? I'm so out of practice with women, I can't really tell. I suppose I *could* read her mind, but that would be cheating. I don't use that particular talent as much as some angels do.

"Are you serious?" Lucy asks. "You're asking me on a date?"

"I am."

"Like a date-date? A *real* date?"

Why does she sound so surprised by this? Am I really that terrible at making my feelings known? "Yes, Lucy. A real date."

"Well, the answer is *yes*... obviously. Followed by a giant *duh*." She glances back at Joe's house, where Sam is watching from the window. "When did you want to go?"

"Anytime."

"How about now?" Lucy suggests. "If we don't go now, I'm afraid you're going to change your mind. Just let me text Sam, and then we can go somewhere... *anywhere*. I don't care where we go, I'm just really, really excited."

Her reaction is adorable, but I'm trying to stay straight-lipped. Lucy is the only girl who can make me smile, but the expression feels unnatural on my lips.

"Where would you like to go?" I ask. "What is the perfect first date according to Lucy Alvarez?"

"The perfect date is anywhere with Archangel Azrael." Her answer has her blushing, so she quickly adds, "Uhh... m-maybe we could have

134

a picnic on the beach? I've always loved the beach. You can collect seashells, build a sandcastle, walk barefoot in the sand. It's nice."

"The beach it is, then!" I declare, warping her to our own private paradise. The snow disappears, replaced by white sands and scattered shells. There is a subtle scent of brine in the air, and a pleasant rush of waves lapping the shore.

"Wow, you picked a good one!" Lucy exclaims. "It's beautiful here!"

The cheesy cliché, *not as beautiful as you are*, comes to mind, but I can't bring myself to use a phrase so trite. I simply nod, manifest a picnic basket, and choose a spot on the ground. I wonder what she's thinking right now? I really *don't* read her mind too often, but I indulge myself in a peek of her thoughts.

What if Archangel Azrael was my boyfriend? That would be craaazy. Should I wear a swimsuit? I don't know... I don't look good in swimsuits. What if it turns him off?

She joins me on the checkered picnic blanket and says, "I feel like I should be wearing a swimsuit, but I *hate* bikinis. They make me feel naked and my butt looks big."

Her self-assessment is way off. I've always thought she had a perfect bottom. "Wear whatever makes you comfortable, love," I tell her.

"Aww... did you just call me *love*? That's cute." Lucy manifests a pink one-piece and matching sarong. "I'm wearing this to cover my booty. I hope you don't mind."

"Why on earth would I mind? As I said, you should wear what's comfortable." I flip open the picnic basket's lid and extract its contents. There's fried chicken, fresh fruit and potato salad. "If you don't like these options, you're welcome to manifest something else."

"Dude, this looks *gross*. All of it." Amused by my sour expression, she bursts into a fit of giggles. "Oh my god, I'm just messing with you! It looks really good."

"I'm glad you approve."

Lucy plucks one of the grapes from its vine and pitches it through her lips. As she chews, she asks, "How did you know that grapes are my favorite fruit? Have you been reading my mind?"

"Not at all. I *never* read your mind," I lie. I *do* read her mind, I just don't do it often. "It was a lucky guess."

Lucy responds with an incredulous, "Uh huh," and goes back to eating her grapes.

I have little interest in food, but I don't want to be a spoilsport, so I eat some of the potato salad.

"So... if this is a date, we're supposed to take some time to get to know each other better," Lucy says. "Who is your favorite artist?"

I answer quickly, "Picasso... but only because I was his spirit guide once."

"Really? That's cool." Lucy taps her chin and concocts other questions to spring on me. "What is... your favorite band?"

"Beggar's Tongue." She looks a bit clueless, so I add, "It's Archangel Haniel's band."

"Ah. I guess that makes sense."

I fire a question at her before she can ask another one. "What's your favorite movie? You seem to enjoy a lot of them."

"Are you serious? Ugh, that's such a hard question!" Lucy facepalms until the answer comes to her. "I think... maybe... okay, this is going to sound incredibly lame, but I really like the movie *Toy Story*. It was the first movie I ever sat down to watch with my parents, and it felt like a magical moment. I swear, I *do* like some adult movies too." Lucy groans at her word choice. "By *adult movies*, I don't mean porn, I mean movies for adults."

Chuckling, I assure her, "I knew what you meant."

For the next few minutes, we toss random questions back and forth at each other. I learn that her favorite color is blue, her favorite animal is a cat, and her favorite band is, "too embarrassing to admit because it's a boy band." When we finish eating, she jumps up and starts collecting seashells.

"How can I pick these up?" Lucy asks. "Is this some kind of... spirit beach?"

"It is." Every time she bends over to collect a shell, I resist the urge to check out her bottom. She can hate it all she wants, but I think she has a lovely bottom.

"Ooo, jackpot!" Lucy picks up a starfish and holds it up for me to see. "You know, it's *really* cool that we have this entire place to ourselves. I like having our own private beach."

"As do I." I wish I could think of something flirty to say, but I've always failed at the art of flirtation. I tend to be a lot more direct with my emotions, and even then, I keep a lot inside myself. I'm too nervous to tell her how much I like her, or how much I crave her company, or how much her presence illuminates my soul. The world looks brighter when I'm with her.

"Okay, time to build a sandcastle!" Lucy declares. "You build one too. Whoever builds a better castle gets to decide what we do on our second date."

"Is that so?" I ask, raising an eyebrow. "Is this your subtle way of asking me for a second date?"

"Maybeeee." She smiles cheekily. "Would it be so bad if it was? Besides, you have a lot of movies to catch up on! And we haven't even started talking about tv shows yet..."

Lucy plops down and starts scooping wet sand into a bucket. She hasn't set any rules, so I manifest my entire castle in less than thirty seconds. It has a moat, windows, and tiny, detailed turrets.

When she realizes what I've done, she punches my arm. "Hey, that's not fair! That's cheating!"

"I don't think so," I quietly object. "I did have to visualize it, after all."

"It's still cheating. If you're going to be like that, two can play at this game." Lucy closes her eyes, grins, and manifests a castle that's two times larger and more elaborate than mine. Hers has castle walls wrapping around an immense keep.

"I think you win," I tell her.

"I think I did too... if only because yours looks a little generic." Feigning disappointment, she says, "You know, I expected better from the Angel of Death. I really did."

If I was a little bit braver, I might tickle her for saying something like that. But I'm not brave. Far from it.

After simultaneously demolishing our castles, we decide to walk along the shore, where the sand is damp and waves occasionally brush our feet. Lucy insists on the removal of my shoes, so I humor her.

"I'm from LA, so I went to the beach all the time," Lucy says. "It was one of my favorite places in the world."

"Mine too."

"Cool." Lucy extends an arm, and for a moment, I wonder if she's reaching for my hand. Unfortunately, I'm wrong, and her arm drops back to her side. "So... where should we go on our second date? Any ideas?"

"You were the winner of our sandcastle war, so it's your decision," I remind her. "Also, it should probably wait until you've completed your Helper training. That would be the professional thing to do."

"Okay. How much longer is my training going to take?"

"Not long." When a wave almost knocks her over, I offer her an arm. Her fingers clutch my wrist as she balances herself. "I think you've made a lot of progress. You know how to do the job, I just want to teach you a few more techniques."

"Like what?"

"You'll find out tomorrow. I have a unique mission planned for you."

"Ugh. I hate when you're cryptic!" Lucy complains. "I wish you'd just come out and tell me stuff."

The breeze catches her hair, making a tornado of dark tendrils. As she restrains the flyaway strands, I catch myself staring at her lips. Lucy has beautiful lips, and for the hundredth time, I imagine what it would be like to kiss them. Is it too soon? If I leaned toward her and tried to steal one, would she reject me?

If people knew how timid I was, it would kill my reputation.

"So... just so you know, I like you," Lucy blurts.

"Good." Grinning like a little boy, I add, "Just so you know, I like you too."

"Good." This time, she *does* reach for my hand. My fingers are happily captured by hers. "Now that I know that... it's a huge relief."

Chapter Twenty-Seven: Lucy

AZRAEL LIKES ME. I'm anchored to my bed, as giddy as can be, and I can't think about anything but him. *He likes me. He likes me.* It sounds unreal, even to me. I want to tell Sam about it, but a part of me still can't believe this is happening.

I *actually* went on a date with the Angel of Death. How many girls would want to trade places with me right now? Thousands, I'm sure. How did I get so lucky? There's nothing about me that's even remotely special. I guess I'm a decent-looking, moderately intelligent, occasionally humorous person, but I'm certainly not special. I never thought I would be attractive enough for Archangel Azrael.

I crush a pillow against my face and giggle into the fluff. I'm supposed to be meeting him for our final mission together, but how am I supposed to keep it together? He wants us to be professional until my training is over. I can do that, right?

When I get a text from him, I sit up and compose myself with a few deep breaths. Disappointment crawls into my stomach as I read his words.

Meet me on the Hill of Black Roses.

Wow, that's such a direct, impersonal message. But what did I expect? I don't think Azrael would ever be the type of guy who would send flirty texts. If he did, I would be blown away.

I head to the Hill of Black Roses. Here, we met for our first mission. Here, we're meeting for our final mission. I don't know if I should be happy or sad. On one hand, if my training is over, we're free to date. On the other hand, I wish I could go on missions with him forever.

As I climb the hill, I greet him with an exuberant wave and a beaming smile. He's wearing a plain black t-shirt and khaki pants. Simple as his attire may be, I swear he's never looked more gorgeous. Guys don't have to try too hard to look gorgeous, do they? It isn't fair. I could wear my cutest dress, and I still wouldn't come close to him.

"Hello, Lucy," he greets me. "You look pretty today."

His compliment *almost* makes me giggle. I have to stop the nervous laughter before it squeaks out of me. "Thanks. That's really nice of you. You look handsome too."

Azrael doesn't accept my compliment, he just starts talking again. "When I said we had a unique mission today, it was no lie. Part of our mission as Helpers is to console grieving loved ones who were left behind. Obviously, they can't see us, but there are ways we can reach out to them. You've been concerned about your family, haven't you?"

"My dad and brother? Yeah, I've been really concerned. They'd already lost Mom, and I'm pretty sure my death pushed them deeper into depression." I've been that depressed before. It's almost impossible to claw your way out of it.

"With your permission, I would like to help you make contact with your father and brother," Azrael says. "We will leave subtle clues to let them know you're still around and watching over them."

"We can do that?"

"Absolutely."

"So, basically... we're haunting them?"

Azrael chuckles at my word choice. "No, not exactly. Hauntings, in a traditional sense, are done by shadowlings and negative entities. Spirits have a more subtle approach. I'll give you some ideas when we get there. Warp us."

I take Azrael to my old bedroom, which hasn't been touched since my death. A quick spin around the house confirms that we're alone. Dad and Luis aren't around right now.

I tell Azrael, "Dad's probably at work. Luis is... well, I don't know where he is. Maybe he's out looking for a job?"

Azrael stands in front of a wall of family pictures and crosses his arms. There are pictures me of as a child, pictures of me with grandma, pictures of me dressed up for Halloween, pictures of me on vacation. Basically, there are a *lot* of pictures of me. There are more pictures of me than Luis, that's for sure. Luis always hated pictures. I'm not a fan of them either, but Mom always liked to take them. I guess I was her favorite.

"I propose..." Azrael pauses to wag a finger at the wall of photos. "I propose that we knock off all the pictures of you."

"*No!*" I cry, whacking his arm. "That's too way creepy! I don't want them to come home and get freaked out."

"I'm kidding. Well... mostly kidding. If we did that, it would certainly send a message, wouldn't it?" Pointing at one of the many pictures of me, he says, "You were a cute child."

"No, I wasn't!" I disagree. "I had bad haircuts and braces and a cheesy smile. I was as awkward as a kid could get."

"Still cute," he insists. "Anyway, let's find your father first. Come on."

We locate Dad in a diner with three unfamiliar guys, presumably his coworkers, because they're all wearing the same uniform. The three men are having a lively conversation about recent deaths on television shows, but my dad doesn't seem interested in participating. He's quietly picking through his french fries, looking depressed. Even though he had time to prepare for my death, he hasn't been coping well.

"I'm going to teach you a way to make contact with a loved one without scaring them. It's my favorite method," Azrael says. "Think of something you and your father used to say to each other. Preferably, it has to be something *you alone* would have said to him."

"I used to tell him he looked like Oscar Isaac." My answer seems to confuse him, so I add, "He's an actor in Star Wars. One of my nicknames for Dad used to be Poe Alvarez."

"I have no idea what that means, but we can probably work with it," Azrael says. "Maybe you could get one of these gentlemen to make the comparison?"

"Nah." I reject his idea with a sneer. "It would be better if I got the waitress to say it. Look, here she comes."

The waitress is an attractive redhead in her twenties. If she compares him to a celebrity, he might think she's hitting on him. Dad needs this. She's about ten years too young for him, but maybe she'll give his ego a boost.

The hot waitress asks, "How's your food tasting?" Various mumbled replies by Dad and his co-workers provide an answer to her question. "Can I get you boys anything else?"

I don't have much time—I have to get through to her before she leaves the table. Hopefully she'll know who Oscar Isaac is.

"Tell him he looks like Oscar Isaac!" I yell at her. *"You've seen Star Wars, right? Doesn't the guy with the brown hair totally look like the actor who plays Poe?"*

Oblivious to my shouting, Dad asks the waitress, "Can I get a bowl of vegetable beef soup to go?"

"Sure thing." Her eyes linger on his, so I try yelling at her again.

"Oscar Isaac, the actor from Star Wars! They look alike, don't they? Tell him!"

"Hey..." The waitress hesitantly points at Dad and asks, "Has anyone ever told you you look like that actor from the newer Star Wars movies? The pilot guy. I forget his name..."

"Yeah," Dad answers with a hollow chuckle—the kind of chuckle that has no mirth behind it at all. "His name is Oscar Isaac, and my daughter used to say that all the time."

"That's cool," the waitress says. "Well, you really do look like him, especially in the eyes. Anyway, I'll be back with your soup and your check in a moment."

When I glance at Azrael, he gives me an approving nod. "Well done, Lucy. You got him thinking about you."

"Yeah, but it doesn't actually prove anything to him. He might just think it's a weird coincidence."

"Perhaps. Or he could choose to see it as a sign that his daughter is still with him," Azrael says. "Either way, the gentlemen at his table seemed to enjoy it."

Azrael's right about that. Ever since the waitress walked away, they've been saying she's "into him" and "totally flirting with him." When they start talking about how hot she is, I feel bad for using her to get my message across.

Azrael warps us to my brother's location next, and I feel a little sick when I realize he's sleeping in his ex-girlfriend's apartment. She was controlling, manipulative and unfriendly. I never got along with her, and if my death played a part in driving Luis back into her arms, I'll never forgive myself.

I mumble out loud, "At least I don't have to see her."

One of Azrael's black eyebrows snaps up. "Huh?"

"Luis' ex-girlfriend. I never liked her, so I'm glad she's not around." A quick glimpse at a clock makes me chuckle. It's 12:45. "Why is Luis still sleeping at noon? He used to be an early riser, now he's a lazy riser."

Azrael's answer makes me feel terrible. "He's probably depressed because he lost his sister. It's actually good that he's sleeping, because we're going to attempt to make contact with him... in his dreams."

"We can do that?"

"Only a handful of spirits have learned how to enter mortals' dreams. Even among angels, it can be a rare talent. It requires heavy concentration and an understanding of human brainwave patterns. I've undergone the training, so I can send you into Luis' dream... but only if you want to."

"Will I be able to talk to him?" I ask.

"Definitely. However, he may or may not remember your interactions within the dream. Either way, it could heal some of the ache in his heart." Azrael reaches for my hand and says, "Give me a moment."

Azrael's eyes are closed, so I take a chance to study him. He has to be one of the handsomest guys I've ever seen. One day, I want to hold his face in my hands and touch those delectable cheekbones of his. I want to lean in and kiss the—

"I can hear your thoughts right now," Azrael interrupts me. "If you can, clear your mind. I need to focus on Luis."

Did he really just hear my thoughts about the cheekbones and the kissing? Crushing humiliation burns through every inch of me. I don't want to enter Luis' dream right now! I would rather find a place to hide—and never show my face again.

"You needn't be embarrassed," Azrael says. "Also, you haven't cleared your mind yet."

I take a deep breath and try to make my mind as blank as I can.

...

All of a sudden, the scenery changes. His girlfriend's apartment has been replaced by an open field, with only a single tree to break up the monotony of endless green grass. Luis is sitting under the tree—but it's not the Luis I remember. He looks like he's eight years old again. I barely recognize him.

"Umm..." Turning to Azrael, I ask, "Why is Luis a little kid?"

"My best guess is that he feels helpless and hopeless. His subconscious mind took him back to a form where he felt more safe,"

Azrael explains. "You can still talk to him. He's still your brother... albeit in a smaller form."

Little Luis starts murdering ants with a stick, so I run forward and wrench it from his hand. "No, don't do that! That's bad!"

"Sorry." Luis blinks at me a few times before asking, "Hey, are you my sister?"

"I am." I toss his stick and crouch on the ground beside him. "I wasn't sure you'd recognize me."

"Why wouldn't I recognize you? What a weird thing to say." My little older brother manifests another stick and starts prodding the mud with it. "You know... I haven't forgiven you for leaving me."

"It's not like I had a choice," I whisper. "I was sick."

"I know." Luis turns away, probably to hide the tears in his eyes. He never liked to cry in front of people. "Until you died, I think I was in denial. I didn't actually think I'd lose my little sister. I kept thinking you'd get better, or... I don't know. I didn't accept that it was going to happen until a few days before your death. I feel like an idiot."

"I always knew I was going to die. As soon as the doctor gave me the diagnosis, I had this awful feeling in the pit of my stomach. I felt like he was talking to someone else... someone who wasn't me. It was so unreal."

"What's it like to be dead?" Luis asks.

"It's not so bad. I get to hang out with cool people like Archangel Azrael." I thrust a thumb at the handsome man standing beside me.

Luis rubs the gloss from his eyes before facing Azrael. "He doesn't look like an angel. He doesn't even have wings."

"Well, he *is* an angel," I insist. "Also... I miss you like crazy, big brother."

It's strange to call him *big brother* when he's in this form, but I'll take what I can get.

"I miss you too," Luis says. "I miss you all the time. Everything I see reminds me of you. Every show I watch... every song I hear. I'm..." He gets choked up and pauses to take a breath. "You were my best friend, Lucy. I wish I would've died first."

"You were my best friend too." Squeezing his tiny shoulder, I tell him, "But I want you to be happy, and I want you to know I'm okay. Mom's okay. Heaven's like a big fiesta, so you don't have to keep worrying about us."

"I love you." Luis suddenly throws his arms around me and sobs into my shoulder. "I wish I would've told you that while you were still alive. You were the best sister in the world. I didn't have you for long, but I was lucky to have you for as long as I did. You... you're a really special girl, Luciana."

"And you were an awesome brother." I hold onto him as tight as I can and cry like a baby. "I'll always watch over you, okay? Always, always. Never forget that."

Through his sniffles, Luis says, "I know this is a dream. I wish it was real."

My lips aren't far from his ear, so I whisper my reply.

"How do you know it isn't?"

Chapter Twenty-Eight: Azrael

I'VE MET ABRAHAM LINCOLN, Mother Teresa, and Martin Luther King Jr. I taught Robert the Bruce how to be an Archangel. I used to hang with Jimi Hendrix when he was a part of Haniel's band. None of these legends made me half as nervous as Luciana Alvarez's mother.

Now that her training is over, Lucy doled out a mission to me. I'm supposed to convince Mrs. Alvarez that Lucy has what it takes to be a good Helper. While I'm at it, I'm going to ask for permission to court her daughter. That might sound old-fashioned to someone like Lucy, but the last time I dated a young lady, getting permission from a parent was required, and the girl was often accompanied by a chaperone. Perhaps I'm stuck in the past? I need to upgrade my dating habits.

Conchetta Alvarez is an intimidating lady. As soon as she sees me, her eyebrows snap together to form a disapproving glare.

"Well... he's handsome, I'll give him that," Conchetta says. "Isn't it unusual for an Archangel to visit his student at her home?"

"It *is* unusual. But Lucy is a very special student," I reply.

My eyes lock on Luciana, who's standing behind her mother. She winces when Conchetta asks, "*How* is she special?"

"Mom!" Lucy whines. "Don't put him on the spot like that!"

"No. It's alright." A pale brown dog decides to crash on my lap, so I give him a few light pats on the head.

"That's Poncho," Lucy identifies the scraggly terrier, giving me a reprieve from her mother's question. "He likes strangers more than he likes us, I swear."

As I massage Poncho's head, I say, "You know how Archangels can hear a person's thoughts? Well... we can hear animal thoughts too."

"Oh *really?*" Lucy crosses her arms and challenges me, "In that case, what is Poncho thinking right now?"

"He's thinking..." I close my eyes and take a deep breath as I prepare to reveal the canine's innermost thoughts. "He's thinking *ruff ruff... ruff ruff ruff... rowl.*"

Lucy gasps at my answer ."Oh my god... did Archangel Azrael *actually* crack a joke? That's a first."

"Oh, I wasn't joking. I'm absolutely serious," I insist, grinning impishly. "Unfortunately, I have no idea what it means. I don't speak dog."

Lucy's right. I don't crack jokes too often. I like to think I have a fairly decent sense of humor, but my delivery is poor. It's usually too dry or too monotone.

"*Excuse me!*" Conchetta speaks up. "You said my daughter is special. I'm still waiting to find out *why* you think she's special. I think she's special too, but I want to hear what you have to say. And why should she be a Helper?"

This time, my answer rolls from my tongue. "Lucy is bright, sweet and determined, and she's wise beyond her years. She empathizes with her charges in so many ways. She's a personable young woman, very easy to talk to... and she even got me to open up to her. Even though she's been through some tough times, she radiates with so much light, she spreads it to others around her." Lucy's cheeks are overrun by shades of pink as I praise her. She's blushing, and it's adorable. "Also... she has the prettiest smile in the world, the cutest laugh I've ever heard, and I wish I could work with her for one more day."

"I wish *I* could work with *you* for one more day!" Lucy echoes the sentiment. "Why couldn't we work together on a mission someday?"

Lucy's mom jumps in before I can answer. "Why do Helpers have to work alone? It sounds like a stressful job as it is. Why must they be lonely too?"

"It's just the way it's always been, ma'am. It's—"

She interrupts again. "That isn't an answer. It's a cop out."

"Mom..." Lucy groans into the palm of her hand. "Can you give him a break? Please?"

"Not if he doesn't answer my question!" Conchetta says.

I try to flesh out my answer for Conchetta. "In the mortal realm, people are always dying. *Always.* Helpers are in high demand. There aren't as many of us as there could be."

"So? Here's a solution for you! Hire more of them. If you add more Helpers, maybe they could team up?"

Lucy's mother is an outspoken lady with unwavering opinions. I think it's refreshing. Not many people are brave enough to argue with an Archangel.

"I'll consider that," I tell her.

"Good. Now I'm going to manifest some of my homemade chocolate chip cookies," Conchetta says. "I challenge you to find a better cookie in the entire world."

A mountainous pile of cookies suddenly appears on the table in front of us.

"*Eat,*" Conchetta demands. "They're hot and gooey too, just the way Lucy likes them."

I sample one of the cookies, and as I chew, I give her a thumbs-up.

"They're delicious, aren't they? Of course they are!" Conchetta exclaims. "Now... what were you saying about Lucy's pretty laugh and cute smile? If I didn't know any better, I would think you had a crush on her."

"*Moooom!*" Lucy really stretches out the word as she whines yet again. "Oh my god, you are *so* embarrassing today!"

"You could say, I suppose, that I have a crush on her." Personally, I think the word *crush* is too small to describe my feelings, but I keep that thought to myself. "I admire her very much."

"Admire her... or *like* her?" Conchetta asks.

In the corner of my eye, I can see Lucy's face diving into the palm of her hand.

"I like her," I admit. "In fact, I was hoping I could ask for your permission to date her."

"Permission? Why would you need my permission?" Conchetta swats my arm so hard, I almost drop my cookie. "If an Archangel wanted to date my daughter, I would be jumping for joy! I do have one more question, though. Didn't you fire her once? *Why?*"

"Because I liked her too much." My gaze drifts back to Luciana, whose face is an even more violent shade of pink than it was before. "I was afraid of liking her too much. To be honest, I... hadn't liked anyone for a very long time."

Conchetta asks, "Isn't that what Archangel Jophiel used to say when he wanted a woman to like him?"

Poor Jophiel. After his trial, everyone seems aware of his scandalous past. I wonder if he'll ever be free of that reputation? "Jophiel's technique was... somewhat similar. But in my case, it isn't a lie. I've chosen to be single for a very long time."

"And Lucy is the girl who's going to end that for you? That's nice. That's—"

Lucy doesn't let her mom finish the thought. She gives her an impassioned lecture in Spanish and pleads for a change of subject.

"How about we watch a movie, then?" Conchetta suggests. "Lucy said you were a fan of movies."

"I actually *didn't* say that," Lucy corrects her. "Mama... this just proves you never listen when I talk, because I actually said the opposite. Azrael *doesn't* like movies and he thinks they're a waste of time."

"Actually, I would be happy to watch a movie, Mrs. Alvarez," I speak up. "What movie did you have in mind?"

"My favorite."

Lucy groans at her mom's answer. "No, Mom. Please don't make Archangel Azrael watch *Dirty Dancing*. Please."

"Why not? We could watch the sequel, if you prefer. I don't care what the critics say... I really liked *Havana Nights*."

I want to impress Conchetta, so I assure her that any movie is fine with me. About five minutes into *Dirty Dancing*, Lucy whispers to me, "I've seen this movie, like... twenty times. Mom made me watch it. A lot."

"She must be quite a fan."

"She is. She can quote the whole thing. It's ridiculous."

I silently study the plot, even though it's nothing I would choose to watch on my own. If Lucy and I are going to date, I should expect to watch plenty of movies in my future. She seems to be quite a fan of them.

When the last dance has been danced and the credits roll, Conchetta hugs me twice and makes me promise to visit again. She seems to have accepted the fact that her daughter is going to be a Helper. She may not like it, but she's given up the fight.

Lucy walks me to the door, and for a moment, both of us are quiet. Neither of us knows how to proceed. Lucy has little experience with men, and I've forgotten how to woo a girl. Furthermore, I have very little knowledge of modern dating rituals.

I lean down to kiss her cheek. I wanted to aim for the lips, but I lost my nerve.

"So... I'll hear from you soon?" Lucy asks.

"Yes. I'll be in contact with you about your first solo mission." My reply sounds disgustingly formal. I hate it.

"Good. I'm a little nervous about it."

"Don't be. You'll be fine." I want to touch her cheek or tuck a lock of hair behind her ear. I want to do something besides stand in awkward silence, but I can't. "So, uh... I guess I should dismiss myself?"

"I guess."

She sounds disappointed in me, and I don't blame her. I'm disappointed in me too. I'm the one who should make the next move, but I'm a useless lump. At the very least, I should remind her about our second date, but I don't. I mutter a polite farewell and excuse myself.

Maybe, deep down, I'm still afraid to let this happen? If Lucy was mine, I wouldn't want anything or anyone else.

How is that not a terrifying thought?

Chapter Twenty-Nine: Lucy

FOR MY FIRST SOLO MISSION, I decide to work with Sam at Asylum Seventeen. I'll eventually have to manage my own Asylum, but until it's been assigned to me, I'm free to work wherever I want to work. This morning, I got a list of missions on my LightTab, and *of course* I chose the Asylum Seventeen one. If I can talk to Sam for a little while, it won't feel like I'm so alone.

I really will be *totally alone* on this mission. I have no partner, no help, and no one to monitor my progress. I'll get a mission report at the end of the day, but for the most part, I won't have any contact with anyone.

I meet Sam at Asylum Seventeen's entrance, where he tells me, "Congratulations on officially becoming a Helper... *and* on winning the heart of a certain Archangel."

I want to knock him on the head for saying that. He knows I've been on a date with Azrael, but I've hardly won his heart! If anything, my relationship with Azrael has hit a wall. Rather than lecture Sam, I dive into the mission. "So... there will be a reunion at Asylum Seventeen today?"

"Yeah. One of our residents, a young lady named May, is reuniting with her father today. She parted from her parents more than thirty years ago, so it should be an interesting one."

I've already done my homework on this mission. May was eleven years old when she lost her life in a car accident. Her parents were in their thirties when she died, and now they're seventy-something. May chose to halt the aging process at age eleven, so when they meet her, it will look like she hasn't aged a day.

"Are you sure you're ready for this, Lucy?" Sam asks.

The truth is, I'm *not*. The idea of doing this alone has always been intimidating, but if Azrael thinks I can handle it, I have to try. "Yeah. I'm totally ready," I lie.

"Alright then," Sam says. "Send me a message after Claude dies. We'll need a few minutes to get ready for the reunion."

I give Sam a firm nod, hoping it makes me look confident. I don't feel very confident, but at least I can try to *look* confident. I've hardly mastered warping, but I make it to Southcrest Medical, the hospital where Claude Lacont is hanging on to the last few hours—or minutes—of his life. I find him in Room 404. He's completely unconscious, but his wife is still at his side, gripping one of his pale hands. She's surrounded by crumpled tissues, and her cheeks are slick with tears. I wonder how long she's been crying?

I sit in the corner of the room, watching Bernadette Lacont as she quietly cries. I can't imagine what it would be like to lose a partner after you've been with them for so long. It must be crushing.

I really wish Azrael was here. It feels weird for him *not* to be here. He always tried to cheer up his charges with comforting words, so I try the same thing with Bernadette.

"You'll see him again one day. I know it hurts now, but it'll be okay."

My "comforting words" sound way lamer than anything Azrael used to say. Oh well. At least I tried, right?

"Yours is the kind of love I wish I had," I tell her. "You and Claude are lucky to have each other. We should all be that lucky! I can't imagine being with someone for as many years as you've been with Claude. Losing him will be the hardest thing you've ever lived through, but you're a strong lady. I can tell."

Bernadette's tears stop, so maybe my speech had an effect on her?

It feels like I'm sitting in the hospital for hours, but only forty minutes pass. His heart monitor suddenly flatlines, and even though the hospital staff hurries in to check on him, it's already too late. Claude is standing outside of his body.

I pop out of my chair as soon as I see him. "Hello!" I exclaim—and in my mind, I immediately lecture myself for sounding too cheerful. No one wants to hear a cheerful voice right after they die, do they?

It takes him a moment to respond. "Hel... lo?"

"I'm Luciana Alvarez, one of your spirit guides." I thrust out a hand, but he seems reluctant to take it. "I'm here to take you Home."

"Home?" His eyelashes flutter at the word. "You mean... heaven?"

"Yeah, some people call it that." As we're shaking hands, a doctor pronounces him dead, and his wife shatters with a sob. She strokes her dead husband's hair and cries on his shoulder, gasping for air as she wails.

"Poor Bernadette," I whisper. I suddenly remember that I'm supposed to send a text to Sam, so I type a quick one.

Claude died. Taking him Home soon.

Claude tries to touch his wife, but his hand passes through her. "Do I have to leave her?"

"Unfortunately... yes," I answer with a wince. "But it's not all bad news. I'm going to reunite you with your daughter, May."

In my mind, I criticize every word that comes out of my mouth. I'm sure Azrael would have made everything sound a lot more smooth.

"May..." Tears twinkle in Claude's eyes as he whispers the name of his long-lost daughter. "May's alive?"

"Well, there's been some debate about what the word *alive* means, but yeah... in my world, May's still alive, and she's been missing you. She'd really like to see you. She—"

The lights flicker and buzz, halting my reply. I thought I caught a glimpse of a shadow near the door, but it might've been my imagination. I *hope* it was my imagination.

"I've missed May with all my heart. Her death almost destroyed us," Claude says. "Take me to her. I want to see my little girl again."

Claude doesn't seem concerned about the flickering lights, but then again, he didn't see the shadow moving behind him. The question in my mind is a sickening one.

What if this hospital has demons?

I don't wait around to find out. I would have given Claude a few more minutes to be with his wife, but I need to get him out of here. I take his wrist and try to warp us to Asylum Seventeen.

But I can't. Either I'm so rattled that I've forgotten how to warp, or something is interfering with my abilities.

Claude looks at me like I'm crazy, shakes his wrist free, and tries to touch his wife's hair. He's probably giving her chills with all that touching, but I don't stop him.

I hear a demonic hiss, and it's *way* too close for comfort. I've only encountered a demon once, with Larry, on my fourth mission as a spirit school student. I remember that hissing sound all too well. It's the kind of sound that could make a spine shiver like crazy.

My first instinct is to contact Azrael and tell him what's going on, but I don't want him to think I failed my first mission. At this point in my afterlife career, it would be *way* too embarrassing to admit I couldn't warp. When Larry and I encountered our demon, he had to summon an Archangel with his LightTab—so that's what I do. I pull up a special screen and make a request.

While I'm typing, a spider-shaped shadow drips down from the ceiling and lands on the floor with a *plop.*

"What's *that?*" Claude shrieks—and I feel really sorry for him. This is a terrible first experience as a spirit.

"Claude, we have to get out of here." I tug on his sleeve, but he doesn't budge. "I'm serious. We have to get out of here *fast.*"

"What *is* that?" he asks again.

The spider lunges at him with a clawed leg, restoring Claude's ability to move. We both bolt to the door, screaming as the spider chases us.

"Uh... unfortunately, that's a demon." How am I supposed to sound calm when I'm totally, completely, utterly freaked out myself?

"A demon?" Claude stops in the hall, a few paces from his hospital room. "Maybe I shouldn't leave my wife with that thing? Maybe I should—"

The spider catches up to him and lashes his leg. I hear a grotesque sizzling noise as the claw burns its way through Claude's flesh. I don't let his screaming distract me, and as the spider advances again, I shout, "*Get back!*"

I don't know how, but a stream of silver light suddenly bursts from my hands, knocking back the demon. I grab Claude's arm and drag him along, forcing him to limp to the elevator.

"Shit, that hurt!" Claude cries. I can't bring myself to look at his leg, but I can imagine what it looks like. It's probably black and charred.

The elevator doors open with a *ding*, and I shove him inside as fast as I can. I've already made a mess of this mission, haven't I? With trembling hands, I check my LightTab's screen. My request for an Archangel is still active, but no one's responded yet. Should I try to contact Azrael directly? If he knew I was in trouble, would he come faster? If he finds out I'm failing, is he going to fire me again? I have so many questions in my mind, my head hurts.

I try to reassure Claude, even though I desperately need someone to reassure me too. "By the way, don't worry about your wife too much. The demons can hurt us, but they can't cause a human any physical harm. They can effect a human's mood... they can make them angry or sad... but it can't hurt Bernadette."

"That's... good to know."

Why does this hospital have demons? Were they tempted by the depression here? Larry said they're drawn to rage and sorrow, and a hospital is probably teeming with those emotions. Or... maybe they've come to feed on the fear of death?

I try to warp two more times, but we're stuck here until the elevator opens. Another demon is waiting for us on the other side of the sliding doors. This one is even more hellish than the last. It's a smoky black mass, roughly the size of a toddler, and it screams when it sees us.

An Archangel appears behind us, pushes us out of the way, and skewers the demon with a thrust of his sword. I don't recognize him, but he's really handsome. He has a boyish face, big eyes, and honey-colored curls.

As soon as the demon is down, the Archangel whirls around and sticks out a hand. "Sandalphon," he introduces himself. "And you don't need to tell me why I was summoned. I think the answer's obvious. There are demons here?"

I reply, "Yeah. That's the second one we've encountered. There's another one on the fourth floor... it's some kind of spider thing."

"Thanks for letting me know. It will be impossible to do a full sweep of a building as big as this. I think I'll check some key areas and come back with a few more Archangels."

I don't know if I'm supposed to follow Sandalphon, but I do, and so does Claude. My poor charge looks *very* confused right now, and he still has a limp. For Claude's sake, I almost ask Sandalphon to take us back home, but I would have to admit that my warping powers are broken, and I can't bring myself to do that.

"Stay close to me," Sandalphon says. "We're going to check the nursery first. Children and babies... they're in more danger from demons than most."

"Why's that?" I ask.

"Sometimes, if the child is young enough, it can actually see the demon. It can be a traumatizing experience," Sandalphon explains. "Besides that, children have more energy, and the demon will feed on as much as it can."

I still wish Azrael was here. Don't get me wrong, I'm glad that Sandalphon showed up, but I wanted *my* Archangel.

Okay... to be fair, Azrael is hardly mine, but it would be nice to have him at my side again.

"You and Azrael are close, right?"

I groan at Sandalphon's question. I keep forgetting to be careful with my thoughts when there's an angel around. I almost launch into a speech about how Azrael and I aren't as close as I want to be, but the sight of six demons milling around the nursery eclipses all other thoughts. They're weaving between cribs, hissing and gurgling.

I'm probably stating the obvious when I say, "That... is awful."

"Indeed it is," Sandalphon agrees. "Stay out here while I take care of the demons. Whatever you do... don't go inside."

Behind a wall of glass, Claude and I watch the Archangel rush into the nursery and carve into one of the demons. When a demon with really long arms tries to grab him from behind, I clap a hand over my mouth. Spindly, smoky fingers clamp down on Sandalphon's shoulder. He spins around, handling the situation before any real damage is done—although I do see a slight black burn on his neck.

"I assume this isn't typical?" Claude asks.

"Nope," I reply. "There's nothing typical about this. You haven't had any of the good experiences of crossing over and... I'm sorry about that."

Does this mean I've failed my first mission as a Helper? Looking at Claude's scorched leg, it certainly feels like a failure. There's also the fact that I can't seem to warp anymore. At this point, I wouldn't blame Azrael if he wanted to strip away my Helper status.

My eyes snap up when I hear a creaking noise. Four of the long-armed demons are heading down the hall, but I don't think they've spotted us yet. I try to bang on the wall to get Sandalphon's attention, but my fist just passes through the glass.

"Sandalphon!" I scream his name, but he's still busy with the demons inside the nursery. "Sandalphon!"

Sandalphon doesn't hear my shouting, but the demons definitely do. I have no idea what I'm supposed to do, so I give Claude a shove and yell, "*Run!*"

Claude can't run very fast on his injured leg, and I don't want to get too far ahead of him, so I try to keep his pace. That's a bad idea, because at this rate, the demons *will* catch up to us. Discouraging questions race through my mind. How much damage can a demon do? Can it leave me disfigured? Can they destroy my soul? If I'm attacked, how much will it hurt?

Fortunately, I never have to find out.

Archangel Azrael appears behind us. He swings his massive sword, unleashing a burning red shock wave that rips through all four demons at once. It looks a lot more effective than anything Sandalphon can do.

I'm tempted to throw my arms around Azrael, crush my face against his chest, and express my gratitude in kisses, but I don't do any of that. All I can say is, "Thanks."

I guess that's not enough for Azrael.

He wraps his arms around *me* and whispers, "I'm never leaving you again."

Chapter Thirty: Lucy

AS CLAUDE EMBRACES the daughter he hasn't seen in over thirty years, my mind drifts to other matters. Did I fail my first mission as a Helper? Am I going to be fired again? I'm afraid to know the answer, and Azrael's unmoving lips don't provide any clue. He was relieved to see me safe, but that doesn't mean he isn't disappointed in me.

On the plus side, Claude's leg seems to be healing. Sam and two other angels from Asylum Seventeen wrapped it in some kind of magical cast, and less than a minute later, his leg was almost normal again.

"It's not your fault," Azrael whispers to me.

"Hm?"

"The demons' attack," he clarifies. "It wasn't your fault, Lucy. You couldn't have known they would be there, and it isn't as if you could fight them off on your own. You handled the situation well, all things considered."

But I couldn't warp. I haven't mentioned that to Azrael yet, but I'm sure he already knows. If I could have gotten us out of the hospital, Claude wouldn't have been attacked.

Azrael suddenly manifests a big box of Reese's Pieces and passes it to me. "For you," he says. "I thought you might need it after the day you've been through."

The candies rattle as I clutch the box to my heart. "Aww, I think that's the sweetest thing anyone's ever done for me!"

His brow pinches at my claim. "Really?"

"Seriously. I'm not even kidding," I tear into the box like I'm starving and pour a few pieces into my mouth.

While I'm chewing, Sam drifts over and wraps an arm around me. "I am *so* sorry about what happened to you!" he exclaims. "Are you sure you're going to be alright?"

"Yeah."

"What you went through... it sounds terrifying. And just so you know, I could have given that job to anyone and it could have ended the same way."

It's nice of Sam and Azrael to try to cheer me up, but I still feel like I failed. The image of Claude's charred leg is going to be stuck in my head forever. Someone more seasoned might have been able to prevent that. Someone more seasoned *definitely* wouldn't have forgotten how to warp in the heat of the moment.

Azrael catches my attention with a heavy sigh. "What's up?" I ask him.

"I'm just thinking... I should probably get back to work."

Nuh uh. No way. After all that, he's just going to leave me? "I thought you said you'd never leave me again?" I remind him. Sam, realizing we might be on the verge of a private discussion, excuses himself without a word.

"I might have been exaggerating a bit," Azrael says. "Besides, I doubt you'd want me with you all the time."

Grinning devilishly, I reply, "I can think of worse things."

The Asylum Seventeen volunteers roll out a banquet to celebrate Claude and May's reunion, but I doubt I'll stick around for it. I'm happy enough with my Reese's Pieces.

Azrael says, "If anything, this debacle has forced me to reconsider if it's truly necessary for Helpers to perform their missions alone. It might be safer in teams of two."

"*Exactly!*" I exclaim. "I don't think I would have freaked out even half as much if someone else was with me."

"Maybe *I* could go with you on your next mission?"

I can feel my smile turning giddy when he asks that. He wants to go with me again, doesn't he? He misses going on missions with me. I shouldn't tease him too much, though, because I don't know how he'll take it.

I finally ask the burning question of the day. "So... did I fail?"

"No, of course not. Like your friend Samuel said, that would have been a trying mission for anyone."

"Not for you. You ripped through those demons like butter. It was seriously impressive."

Azrael doesn't respond. I have a feeling he has something else on his mind.

"Lucy," he whispers my name. "If you don't mind, I would like to take you somewhere private."

I clap a hand on his arm and say, "I'm in. Let's go." I hope that doesn't sound too enthusiastic, but I've been dying to be alone with him.

Azrael warps us to the Hill of Black Roses, the first place I met him. I'm still enthralled by the inky black petals on these flowers. I've never seen anything like them.

Azrael says, "You always wondered why I don't grieve for my charges. Well, the truth is... I do. I grieve for them all the time. Many years ago, I started visiting this hill after my missions. Back then, the flowers were a vibrant, bright red. I would sit among the flowers, lost in my thoughts, and over time... my grief altered their hue."

My eyes gape at the revelation. "*You* turned the flowers black?"

"I believe I did," Azrael says. "I would rage, I would mourn... sometimes, if a mission truly bothered me, I would even shed a tear or two."

"Nuh uh!" I exclaim. "There's no way *you* ever cried!"

"But I do cry. For every lost child that's taken from his mother, for every two lovers that are torn apart, I mourn. My heart hurts for them.

Even though I know they'll be reunited one day, I feel their pain... but I bury it. I bury it because I have to." Azrael squats near the flowers and pushes some of the black petals aside. "Look at this, Lucy."

It's not hard to figure out what he wants me to see. Hidden among the black flowers, there's a single red rose.

"I noticed this a few days ago," Azrael says. "For some odd reason, I think the flowers are turning red again."

"Really?" I crouch next to Azrael, to better observe the flower. It certainly stands out among the rest. "Why do you think that's happening?"

"If I had to guess, I would say it's because of you. *You* have given me a reason to be happy again. My existence revolves around death and *only* death. Since I've met you, you'd made it something more than that."

When Azrael rises, I rise with him. I want to say something, but I'm stunned. I had no idea he felt this way about me.

"You've given me something to be happy about, Lucy." Reaching for my hand, he asks, "Do you think you could ever like me, as dull as I am?"

"You're not dull!" I defend him. "And I already like you. I like you a lot."

There's a better word than "like" to describe how I feel about him, but I think I'll save that confession for another day.

"I care about you... more than you know," Azrael says. "When I realized you were under attack, I panicked, and I came to you as fast as I could. I was so afraid you would be hurt, and I was angry with myself for insisting that Helpers should go alone. You will *never* go alone again. I mean it."

I don't want him to think I'm incapable, so I ask, "I'm not the only Helper who's going to need a babysitter, right?"

"No… no, of course not. Starting tomorrow, *all* Helpers will form teams of two." Lowering his voice, he adds, "And I want you on my team."

This is literally my dream come true. If I didn't jump at this opportunity, I'd be an idiot. "Okay. I accept your invitation."

When Azrael goes silent, I feel a little frustrated. I want more than this. Getting cancer at fifteen really stunted me in some ways. I've been waiting eighteen years for my first kiss, and frankly, I don't want to wait another minute. I deserve at least one kiss from the guy of my dreams, don't I?

"Kiss me." The request flies out of my mouth. I'm surprised at myself for being so bold.

Azrael immediately leans down to fulfill my request. I try to be calm, but on the inside, I'm screaming. *It's really going to happen. He's really going to kiss me.* I'm short and he's tall, so he has to bend down a *lot* to reach my lips. Standing on tiptoes doesn't seem to help.

Pleasure tingles through my body when Azrael's lips meet mine. This is officially the most amazing moment of my life, and I'm glad I didn't waste my first kiss on some stupid high school boy. This is *much* better.

I don't just get one kiss from the guy of my dreams. *I get two.* When we finally pull apart, his fingers stay in my hair, sifting through my brown locks.

"You're a beautiful girl, Miss Alvarez," Azrael whispers. "You're beautiful, and you're mine."

"I *am* yours," I agree. "I hope you know… this means you'll be watching a *lot* more movies from now on, right?"

Azrael flinches a bit, but he's smiling, so I don't think I've rocked his world too hard.

"For you," Azrael says, "I would watch all the movies in the world."

His declaration makes me chuckle. "Wow, the Angel of Death is going to be a movie buff now? You've *really* changed."

"I have." As his mouth descends on mine once again, he whispers against my lips, "And it was worth it."

Author's Notes (Part Two)

PREVIOUSLY, I MENTIONED that many parts of this book were based on true stories. One such part is the "Oscar Isaac" chapter.

My mom had a love-hate relationship with my eyebrows. She used to rave over them, often comparing them to Brooke Shields' eyebrows. In her next breath, she would talk about plucking them. (Mom, make up your mind!)

My dad had a slow death, but my mom's death took us all by surprise. I was twenty years old when I lost her. In her last days, my mom had an awesome nurse named Fay, who cried with us and comforted us.

My mom had *just* died, in fact, her corpse was still in the room. Fay, at this strange moment, decided it was necessary to tell me (not once, but *twice!*) that I had "Brooke Shields' eyebrows."

I was so mired in grief that it took me a moment to remember that my mom used to say that. To this day, I'm still stunned when I think of that. Was my mom trying to reach me through Fay?

Thank you, from the bottom of my heart, for reading this book and sticking with this series. Every reader means so much to me! I would like to continue writing the *School for Spirits* series, but I don't know if there's an audience for them. If you would like to read more, please email me at aronlewes@gmail.com or let me know in a review. And if there's any character you would like to see more of, don't hesitate to let me know.

For news on future releases, I also encourage you to sign up for my mailing list: http://eepurl.com/c-PqSH

Also, if you haven't already, grab a free copy of *The Barefoot Barmaid*, written under my pen name Caylen McQueen. I've included a short sample with this book.

Thanks again!

THE BAREFOOT BARMAID - One

"*Raine*!" Kitt's eyes were wide as she stormed into the kitchen where her stepmother, in a sagging blouse, was shamelessly sucking on sticky sweets. A copious amount of cleavage surged from the top of Raine's shirt, and when she licked the chocolate from her fingers, her lips made an unnecessarily loud smacking noise. "Raine, have you seen my slippers?"

"Thank goodness you don't call me *Mama* anymore, girl." Raine ran a finger under her eye, presumably to smooth a tiny wrinkle. "I'm only ten years older than you, you know. When you used to call me *Mama*, it was awkward." The age gap was more like fifteen years, but Raine had a tendency to round down.

"I haven't called you that in ages," Kitt pointed out. "And I don't think I'd call you that again. *Ever.*" Her nose wrinkled as she repeated, "Have you seen my slippers?" Kitt checked herself in the looking glass as she waited for her stepmother's reply—which was delayed by more sweets stuffed into the woman's flabby cheeks. She readjusted her gray newsboy cap, loosened the collar of her tie, and tugged on her shirt ever-so-slightly. For a barmaid, she thought she looked rather posh.

When she finished chewing, Raine kicked up her feet on the table, as if flaunting the fact that she was wearing her stepdaughter's missing footwear. "They're right here on my own two feet. As you can see."

"Well, I need them!" When Kitt tried to grab Raine's foot, her stepmother tucked her feet under the table, out of view. "I have to be at work in less than ten minutes!"

"That's too bad for you, dear. These are mine now. I've commandeered them."

"That's not funny."

"I'm not trying to be funny, Kitty!" Raine threw back her head and laughed, as loudly and snidely as possible. "I'm quite serious. I needed some shoes, so I took yours."

"Well, can I have them back?"

"*Can you have them back*?" Raine leaned forward, resting her elbows against the table as she lit a long cigar. Her tight black ringlets, recently freed from their curlers, bounced as she shook her head. "Aren't you listening? I took them. They're mine. *Mine*. Don't be so selfish."

"*Selfish*?" Kitt shrieked. "How am I being selfish? They're *my* slippers!" And they weren't even fancy. They were simple and gray, with a tiny hole over the little toe.

"And since we're discussing the topic of your selfishness, you've been avoiding a particular issue." Raine took a drag from her cigar before jabbing it in Kitt's direction. "You're nearly twenty, girl. You should think about getting married soon. Or do you intend to be a burden on your poor, dear papa for the rest of your life?"

"*Ha*!" At first, the only answer Kitt could manage was shocked laughter. After taking a moment to gather her thoughts, she replied, "Of course I don't want to burden my father! But couldn't you also say I'm *only* twenty, so there's no need to rush?"

"I wasn't much older than you when I married your father, you know." Raine dragged a hand through her curl-covered head. She looked exhausted, as if she couldn't believe the nerve of the girl. "By the time you are five and twenty, your options will be fewer... and as more time passes, fewer and fewer still. No man wants a wife who's approaching thirty when he could have a young lady of eighteen. It's something to consider." She tapped her cigar against an old copper ash tray as she spoke. "Listen to me. Five years will pass very quickly, and suddenly you'll be a less than desirable option."

"W-well..." Kitt hesitated. She was almost afraid to broach the topic. "What if I have *no* desire to marry? Ever."

"And there it is!" Raine suddenly clapped her hands together. "There's that selfishness I spoke of! I swear, girl, it's as if you have no consideration for anyone but yourself!"

"*You* are the one who stole my shoes!"

"Get out of my sight." Raine tried to wave her stepdaughter away with a flick of her hand. "I don't care to see your face right now... not when my head is throbbing like it is!"

"Hangover again?" As she asked the question, Kitt could practically feel the smug smile spreading across her face. It was hard to have pity for a woman who treated her so reprehensibly. "Well, I guess I'll go to work barefoot then."

"Ah, now there's an idea! And it's the first good idea you've had all day." Raine heckled Kitt as she left the house. "Perhaps it will teach you some damned humility!"

Barefoot and fuming, Kitt slammed the door behind her. As she strolled the dirty streets of Lundun, she swore she could feel the filth seeping into her skin with every step she took. The smog in the sky from all the steam engines was bad enough; now the bottoms of her feet were turning black. Tears glowed in Kitt's eyes as she approached the softly-burning street lamp where she was supposed to meet Tobias. He was already waiting for her, which was no surprise. No matter how punctual she tried to be, Tobias was always the one waiting for her.

"*There* you are!" exclaimed Tobias, as if he had been standing there for ages. When his gaze dropped from her eyes to her feet, Kitt suppressed a groan. "Wait... where are your slippers?"

"Stolen." When she heard the sharp warning whistle from a nearby steam train, she grabbed Tobias' arm and pulled him in the direction of the station. The whistle was to let them know there was little time to board. Maybe she was later than she realized? "They were stolen by my stepmother, no less."

"*Why?*" Tobias' brow furrowed as he sprinted to keep up with her. For someone rather short, his friend could move quickly. "No offense, but your slippers were hardly... quality."

"Every time someone starts a sentence with *no offense*, how do they always end up saying something offensive?" Kitt simultaneously rolled her eyes and sighed.

"But I didn't mean anything by it, Kitt! I sw-swear I didn't! It's not like either of us has got fancy things!" As if to prove his point, Tobias tugged on his tattered red necktie, from which there dangled a tarnished silver pocket watch. "So why *did* your stepmum steal your shoes?"

"I don't know. Why does Raine do anything she does? Probably to make my life miserable." As they climbed aboard the train, she caught two people glancing dubiously in the direction of her feet. "Now she thinks I should get married soon."

"R-r-r-really?" His stammer was intensified by shock. When Tobias sat across from her on the train, his face was flushed. He hoped he wouldn't regret what he was going to say next. "Well... you could always marry m-m-me."

"Oh, Tobias!" Kitt dismissed the idea with a wave of her hand. "You're my best friend! Don't be ridiculous! Wouldn't it be too odd for us to marry? Besides, I'm sure my stepmother plans to marry me off to some rich old man... or... as rich as you can get when you're basically living in the slums." Kitt flexed her dirty toes, which helped to remind her of her dire situation. Her family really was the poorest of the poor. "At least, I *hope* he'll be rich. I need to get out of this squalor."

"Well, if you ever change your m-m-mind, you know I'm always here for you." Tobias didn't dare to confess he was actually hoping to be her husband one day, not when she was so firmly against the idea.

Kitt studied Tobias's face across the table. She could think of worse fates than being married to her best friend. He was cute, at least, even if he was a bit younger than her—by a little over a year. His curly blonde mane was fluffy and wild, and a bit longer than her pixie cut. His face was still very boyish, and consumed by countless freckles. Kitt thought he looked too young and cherubic to be anyone's husband, let alone hers.

"Y-you marry me," Tobias continued. "And we can work at Lucky's forever."

"Yeah. That sounds like the happily ever after of my dreams!" Kitt briefly picked up a newspaper, ignoring the headline in large, bold letters: NOTORIOUS SKY PIRATE EMPLOYED BY ROYAL FAMILY. She leafed through the pages and, finding nothing to catch her interest, she quickly tossed it aside. "I wish you wouldn't even make jokes like that."

"But it's not really a joke." Tobias's shoulders popped into a shrug as he spoke. "Right now, I can't see myself anywhere but Lucky's... not because I love it, but because I don't have a lot of other options."

"But there's got to be something better than *this* life..." Kitt responded quietly, peering through the smudged window as the steam train howled to life. "There's got to be."

Two

"WHAT THE BLOODY HELL is *this*?" Lucky's eyes were almost feral when he pointed at Kitt's bare feet. "Where's your shoes, girl?"

"I... lost them."

"Who the bloody hell loses their shoes?" Lucky took a drag from his cigarette and unkindly blew a billow of smoke in Kitt's direction.

"They were... stolen." Kitt winced as she said it. Explaining how and why they were stolen would be more embarrassing than showing up at her workplace with bare feet.

"*Stolen*?" He flicked his cigarette to the ground and crushed it. "Who the bloody hell goes around stealin' shoes?"

"It was my—"

"I don't bloody care, actually," Lucky interrupted her. "Just go inside and get to work. If it can be avoided, try not to show your dirty, stinkin' toes to my customers. I can't have them thinking my workers is so poor they can't even buy shoes for themselves!"

"Sorry..." Kitt softly murmured as she brushed past Lucky and entered the pub. Her boss was well over six feet tall, had a remarkably unfriendly face, and his forearms were thicker than most thighs. As intimidating as he was, she preferred not to talk to him too long, especially when he was railing at her. When she joined Tobias behind the bar, Kitt's head had sunken shamefully between her shoulders.

"You look s-s-sad," Tobias observed. "Was Lucky giving you hell?"

"He definitely wasn't happy with me." As she stood behind the counter, Kitt's eyes scanned the dark room, briefly absorbing the sea of customers' faces. Even though it was barely noon, some of the men were already loud, raucous, and most likely in their cups. Kitt could tell it was going to be a long, busy, miserable day. She watched Tobias polish mugs for a moment before she finally sighed and said, "Well, I guess I should get to work."

"That couple over there hasn't been served yet." Tobias nodded in the direction of an older lady wearing a red feather boa and plumed turban. The woman was sitting on the lap of a much younger man, whose fake smile was obvious, even from the other side of the room. He apparently wasn't enjoying the company of his older, gaudier mistress. "Go take their order, and I'll make the drinks today." Tobias rolled up his sleeves in preparation.

"Alright." Kitt sighed audibly as she resigned herself to work. She approached the strange couple and asked, with feigned politeness, "What can I get you today?"

"Mmm." The older woman playfully rubbed her nose against her lover's. "What'll you have, Snugglebums?"

"I, uh…" The younger man's already-ruddy face turned an even brighter shade of crimson, from his chin to his ears to his scalp. Kitt assumed he was embarrassed by the public usage of his ridiculous nickname. "I'll have, a, uh… scotch."

"*Bo-ring*!" the woman shrilled as she planted a red lipstick kiss on her lover's left cheek. To Kitt, she said, "I'll have a Highland Fling."

It took Kitt a moment to realize she was talking about a drink. "I… *oh*! Alright. I'll be back with your drinks as soon as I can."

As Kitt made her way back to Tobias, one of the louder patrons slapped her rear end. Such inappropriate behavior from drunken men was hardly uncommon, so she bit her tongue and kept walking.

"Oy!" The man who slapped her called to her. He was roughly forty, and looked as if he hadn't washed his face in ages. "Come 'ere a minute, love. I've got sumfin to ask you." Against her better judgment, Kitt turned to face the man. As much as she would have liked to walk away, she knew it was rude to ignore a customer, and she didn't want to tempt any more of Lucky's ire. When Kitt was facing him, the lewd man grinned. He had such a gap between his front teeth, Kitt wondered if he was missing a tooth. "My name's Grim."

"Alright." Kitt tried to sound as calm as possible. "Is there something I can do for you, Mr. Grim?"

"*Mr. Grim*? Didja hear that, boys?" Grim turned to his two cronies, and the three of them roared with laughter. "Lil' girlie here is addressing me like I was a gentleman! That's real right and proper, that is!"

"If there isn't anything you want, I should really get back to work."

When she started to walk away, Grim reached out to capture her arm. "Oh, there's sumfin I want, all right." As he pulled her toward him, his gap-toothed grin returned. "How's about a kiss for old Grim, eh?"

"Sorry... that's not going to happen." Kitt would have liked to plow her elbow into his chest, or perhaps knock out another of his teeth, but she had to remind herself that he was a customer, and she needed her job.

"Aw. Come on, luv. Give us a kiss." Grim pointed at his grime-covered cheek. The many steam engines installed throughout Lundun hadn't done his filthy face any favors. "Just kiss me right 'ere. Or on me bum. I ain't picky.

"*Leave her alone,*" a sharp male voice chimed in. When Kitt turned her attention to the speaker, her eyes narrowed curiously. He looked to be in his mid-twenties, with olive skin, and messy brown hair half-hidden under a dusty black top hat. He wore black trousers and a gray trench coat, which was so ratty, it had several patches sewn onto it. It looked like a homeless man's coat. He hadn't bothered to wear a shirt, and though his trench coat was closed, a portion of his muscular chest was on display. His shrewd, dark eyes were staring straight ahead, as if he couldn't be bothered to glance in their direction.

"Oi?" Grim cocked his head as he observed the speaker. "Who are you to tell me what to do, son?"

"I *could* be your worst nightmare. So if you were smart, you'd leave the girl alone." The man in the patchwork coat lifted his cigarette to his mouth and narrowed his eyes, never once glancing in Grim's direction.

Grim must have felt at least somewhat threatened, because he released Kitt's arm immediately. As she headed back to the bar, Kitt flashed a slight smile in the direction of her hero, but he was looking down at his cigarette, paying no attention to her. Grim and the stranger exchanged no more words, they simply got back to their drinks and their own business. Kitt breathed a sigh, relieved that an incident was avoided.

"Were those guys harassing you?" Tobias asked when she returned.

"Kind of. It's not a big deal." It wasn't a lie. While working at Lucky's, she had certainly lived through worse. Nevertheless, the tiny hairs on her nape still prickled when she replayed the dialogue in her head. As she started pouring customers' drinks, she asked, "Hey... do you know that man over there? He looks so familiar to me." The next time she glanced in the direction of her rescuer, he was suddenly studying her with great interest. She quickly looked away, blushing furiously.

"Who...?" When Tobias followed her gaze to the gentleman in question, his jaw dropped. "Wait, you mean you *don't* know who that is? He's kind of notorious."

"Well... I mean... he looks familiar, but I—"

"That's Francis Doon. His face has been plastered on wanted posters for as long as I can remember!"

As soon as Kitt heard the name, something clicked in her head. "You mean, that's Francis Doon the Sky Pirate? Are you sure?"

"Yeah. That's him. D-d-definitely."

"Well, should we call somebody? Should we try to get in contact with the authorities? They'd probably like to know there's a wanted criminal here." Kitt felt a bit guilty as she considered turning in the man who rescued her, but she assumed there was a reward for his capture—a reward that she desperately needed.

"You *really* don't pay attention to the news, do you?" Tobias rolled his eyes as he handed her an empty glass. "He's working for the royal family now! If we interfered with whatever he's doing, *we* would be the ones in trouble."

"So they've got pirates working for them?" Kitt's brow furrowed as she continued making drinks. "Isn't that somewhat... unusual?"

"Not really. The royal family's been using privateers for ages... but they usually don't hire someone with a reputation as b-b-black as his."

Kitt wished she had paid more attention to the wanted posters, because she was suddenly curious. "What has he done?"

"They say he slaughtered a whole village once. He burned entire families in their homes. He flays his enemies alive, and when he's done with them, he sticks their heads on pikes and displays them as a warning."

"That's... horrid." A monstrous man was in the same room as her, breathing the same air as her. The thought made her sick to her stomach "Has he killed *children*?"

"I'm pretty sure he has." Tobias and Kitt quietly studied the man in question. At that moment, one of the bustier barmaids, Veronika, was flagrantly flirting with him. She was leaning forward, dangling her overflowing bosom in his face. Oddly enough, the pirate couldn't have looked less interested. And when Veronika tried to touch his hair, Doon immediately dodged her hand. "That's w-w-why it's so controversial. No one wants to believe the king and queen would work with a man like that."

"Your stammer's improved," Kitt suddenly pointed out.

"H-h-has it? My m-mum said the s-same thing." He stuttered through his entire response, as if trying to prove her wrong.

"A sky pirate..." Kitt whispered the words. "You know, it's always been a dream of mine to ride on an airship."

"It has?"

"Yeah." The corners of Kitt's mouth dipped into a frown. "But I'd rather die than be stuck on an airship with a rotten bloke like that."

Three

KITT CHECKED HERSELF in the looking glass, as she always did, before heading off to work. Her short ginger hair was tucked away under a cap. Her full, pink lips were dipping into a permanent frown, and her dark brown eyes were swimming in sadness. "This is life," she whispered to her reflection. "This is all there is. Just this. Every day."

She was feeling more disheartened than ever when she entered the kitchen and saw her stepmother sitting at the table, once again wearing her slippers. "Raine..." Kitt drew a deep breath as she prepared to ask her question. "Do you—"

Her stepmother interrupted. "No! You don't have to say it, girl! I already know what you're going to ask, and the answer is *no*. These shoes are *mine*."

"I was going to ask if you'd even care if I was dead, but I'm pretty sure I know the answer to that as well." Kitt's shoulders collapsed as she made her way to the door. "I'll... see you later."

"Buy yourself some new slippers!" Raine shrilled the suggestion as Kitt was leaving the house. "You make money at that job of yours, right? You might not make much, but what else could you possibly need to spend it on?"

Kitt sighed and closed the door. On feet as bare as the day before, she marched to the street lamp where she was supposed to meet Tobias. Along the way, an enormous black shadow crawled across the ground. Kitt didn't have to look up to know what it was. *An airship.* "Take me with you..." she whispered to the airship's crew. "Somewhere, anywhere, *please*! I can't stand to be here anymore!"

If she was gone, she knew she would miss none of it. *The sound of hissing machinery, their engines grinding and screeching. The smog in the air, choking her lungs, as bits of ash peppered the sky.* Kitt knew her situation was hardly different than anyone else living in the slums of

Lundun, and she was no special case, but she knew she was meant for something else. Something better. She felt it in her gut.

Kitt and Tobias rode the train to Lucky's, as they had so many times before. She feared she would be admonished for showing up barefoot yet again, but Lucky didn't even glance in her direction. She did, however, have the attention of Francis Doon, who was sitting in the pub for a second day in a row. It wasn't particularly surprising, as the pub had many regulars. Even Grim had returned. Nevertheless, something about Doon's unflinching gaze brought a chill to her spine.

"Mr. Dobbs." Kitt approached one of the aforementioned regulars with a groan. He was standing in the corner of the room in his knickers, babbling to himself. This was also hardly uncommon.

"*Did it for the money…*" Dobbs murmured against the wall. "*She was in it for the money, for the money, she was! That's all she was. Used me for that and that and nothing else.*"

"Mr. Dobbs," Kitt sighed as he repeated the raving octogenarian's name. "Will you please sit down? You might disrupt the other customers if you do this."

Dobbs gave his scantily-clad rear end a revolting scratch, then he muttered again, "*The wife only wanted the money. She hadn't a care in the world other than that. You poke someone so many times and you know they're going to crack.*"

"Come on, Mr. Dobbs." Kitt gently took him by the shoulder and led him to one of the nearby tables. "Why don't you sit down right here and I'll bring you a drink or a treat. Is there something you want?"

"Lemonade," Mr. Dobbs was in tears as he uttered the word. "An ice cold lemonade would be good. Extra ice please."

"Alright." Kitt sighed again, because it meant she would have to make a special trip to the ice house just for him. "I'll be back with it as soon as I can, okay?"

As she made her way to the ice house behind the pub, she was intercepted by her friend Tayla. She was one of the other barmaids, just a few years older than Kitt. Lucky preferred Tayla because she had long blonde hair and wasn't afraid to flirt—which, according to Lucky, made his customers happy.

Tayla tossed her golden hair over her shoulder, seized Kitt's arm and whispered maniacally, "Good god he's handsome, in't he?"

"Who?" Kitt was just talking to Mr. Dobbs, so her mind was still on him—though she doubted her friend was referring to the mad old man.

"Dun. The pirate. Whatever his name is!"

"Doon?"

"Yeah, that one." Tayla clasped a hand over her heart and sighed dreamily. "What I wouldn't give for a night with him!"

"I suppose you could always ask for a night with him?" Kitt suggested with a shrug. "He seems like the roguish type. I doubt he'd say no."

"You think so? 'Cause Veronika said she propositioned him last night and the bloke didn't seem interested at all!" Tayla fluffed her hair with her fingers and gazed in the pirate's direction with a predatory look in her eyes. "It's strange though, innit? He might be a challenge, and I *do* like a challenge. I bet he likes it dirty, too. Do you think he likes it dirty?"

"Well... good luck with that!" Kitt didn't have a tremendous amount of experience with men—in fact, she had *none*—so she didn't have much to offer to the conversation. "I've really got to get back to work, Tayla. I'll see you later." As she parted ways with her friend, she sent a furtive glance in the direction of Doon. Until Tayla said something about him, Kitt never really thought of him as handsome, but she supposed he wasn't entirely unappealing. Either way, considering his reputation, he wasn't someone with whom she cared to interact. In fact, she planned to go out of her way to avoid him.

Kitt's trip to the ice house was interrupted once again, this time by Tobias. "K-K-K-Ki-Kitt." He stuttered her name so badly, even his ears were blushing in frustration. "You look upset. Do you need my help with anything?"

"I'm quite alright, Tobey, thank you." She briefly forced a smile onto her lips and kept walking. She hoped she wasn't too dismissive because she knew she was lucky to have a friend like Tobias. He was a young man of unfailing kindness, and she appreciated him for that. Lately, however, she found it difficult to appreciate much of anything.

Kitt exited the pub via the back entrance and continued toward her destination. The ice house was just outside, but she was intercepted yet again.

"*Turn around slowly, girl. You try anythin', you're dead.*"

Kitt suddenly felt icy cold metal pressed against the back of her neck. Obeying the speaker's command, she slowly turned until she was facing him.

"Grim." Her voice crackled nervously as she addressed him by name. "I have no idea what you're planning, but you don't want to do this."

"See, that's where yer wrong." He kept his sword pointed directly at her throat as he bared his teeth and plucked a bit of spinach from the crooked bottom row. "I *do* want to do this. I most certainly do!"

"But... surely it's not worth the consequences?" Despite her racing heart, Kitt tried to calmly talk him down. She didn't even know what he was planning, but she knew it couldn't be good. "*I'm* not worth the consequences."

"Wrong again," Grim barked at her. When he leaned closer to her, she could smell the stench of hard alcohol on his breath. "Now... take off yer clothes."

"I'm not going to do that."

"You are." He ran his blade along the collar of her button-down shirt. "You are, because you ain't got a choice, do you?"

"I do have a choice, actually." Kitt raised her chin defiantly. "I *could* let you kill me first."

"Would you rather I strip you?" Grim hissed. "I'm letting you do it yerself because I'm trying to do it gentle."

"Please... don't do this." Kitt kept scanning the area, searching for a way out of her predicament. But the alley was narrow, and he was too close for her to make a run for it. If she survived the day, she made a promise to herself to start concealing a dagger under her clothes. "I don't think you've given this a great deal of thought."

"Oh, I have alright. I've been thinking about how nice and perky your breasts must be." Grim licked his lips at the thought. "Now... off with them clothes! You don't want to make me wait. I'm not happy when I have to—"

Before he could finish his thought, a blood-stained blade suddenly appeared in the center of his chest. Someone was standing behind Grim, and they had run him through.

"Farewell, Shitheel," a menacing voice whispered. There was an awful squelching noise as Kitt's rescuer yanked his blade from Grim's body. Grim, who was hissing his last breaths, dropped to his knees. When he fell, he was promptly kicked aside by Francis Doon, who stepped forward and offered a hand to Kitt. "Are you alright?"

"I... well... I... yes. I think so." Her first instinct was to back away from him, but she was frozen. He had come to her rescue twice now, and for that, she was grateful. But he had just killed a man in front of her. Even if he didn't have the reputation of a seasoned criminal, she might have been afraid of him.

Doon nonchalantly whipped a handkerchief from the pocket of his coat and used it to swab the blood from his blade. As he studied the cloth's stain, he was momentarily awed. Satisfied, he lowered his saber and held out his hand again. "Let's go then, Princess. Shall we?"

"*Princess*?" Kitt's nose wrinkled as she repeated the word. She wondered if it was supposed to be a nickname, or some snide term of endearment. Either way, it didn't suit her.

"Yes, Your Highness. The short hair is a terribly insufficient disguise." Suddenly, the pirate threw an arm around her waist and pulled her toward him. "Now, if you don't mind, I'm taking you home. Don't struggle."

Also by Aron Lewes

A Family of Wizards
Wizard of the 80's
Renaissance Witch
A Modern Warlock

Cinderella & Dragons
After Cinderella
Sleeping Beauty Is Just Not That Into You
The Wicked Witch's Prince

First Contact
Little Alien on the Prairie
Little Alien Enslaved

Magic Dreams
The Wishing Princess
A Noble Queen

My Lady Robin Hood
Lady of Locksley
A Sheriff's Redemption
The Lion Returns

Spirit School
School for Spirits: A Dead Girl and a Samurai
School for Spirits: Final Test
School for Spirits: Rebel Archangel
School For Spirits: Angel of Death
School For Spirits: Archangel Undercover
School for Spirits: Almost an Archangel
School for Spirits: Earth Angel

The Black Knight Chronicles
The Darkest Knight
The Laziest Mage
The Bloodiest Daughter

The Darker Ages
The Darker Ages
The Darker Ages 2: Rebirth
The Darker Ages 3: Retribution

The Fox and the Assassin
Vixen's Chosen
Vixen's Magic
Vixen's Challenge

The Wicked Wizard of Oz
A Farm Boy in Oz
A Farm Boy in Emerald City

Standalone
Cinderella & Dragons
The Darker Ages: The Complete Series
Aurora Abroad
The Black Knight Chronicles: The Complete Series
Machine Rebel
A Farm Boy in Oz: The Complete Series
The Ghost of Redemption (A School for Spirits Story)
Angels & Dreams